The Martyr's Victory

Emma Leslie Church History Series

Glaucia the Greek Slave
A Tale of Athens in the First Century

The Captives
Or, Escape from the Druid Council

Out of the Mouth of the Lion
Or, The Church in the Catacombs

Sowing Beside All Waters
A Tale of the World in the Church

From Bondage to Freedom
A Tale of the Times of Mohammed

The Martyr's Victory
A Story of Danish England

Gytha's Message
A Tale of Saxon England

OSRIC HOLDS THE DOOR

Page 86

EMMA LESLIE CHURCH HISTORY SERIES

The Martyr's Victory

A Story of Danish England

BY

EMMA LESLIE

Illustrated by
W. S. STACEY

Salem Ridge Press
Emmaus, Pennsylvania

Originally Published
1886
Religious Tract Society

Republished 2007
Salem Ridge Press LLC
4263 Salem Drive
Emmaus, Pennsylvania 18049

www.salemridgepress.com

Hardcover ISBN: 978-1-934671-08-5
Softcover   ISBN: 978-1-934671-09-2

PUBLISHER'S NOTE

In *The Martyr's Victory* Emma Leslie uses humble characters to teach us valuable lessons about what true devotion to God looks like. Osric, a monk, knew that it was very likely that he would die in his attempt to witness to the savage Danes but he courageously went anyway. Throughout history countless Christians have done the same, spreading the gospel of Jesus Christ. In the life of Elswitha, a young Christian woman, we are challenged by her willingness to forgive and serve those who have done her great harm, an important lesson for Christians in all ages.

May each one of us be inspired in our faith and devotion to God and be willing to risk everything for the sake of our Lord Jesus Christ!

Daniel Mills

October, 2007

PREFACE TO 1891 EDITION

I must say a few words by way of introduction to this book. My readers must bear in mind that the story is of missionary life in the ninth, not the nineteenth century; and the people sought to be civilized were our own Danish forefathers—"a filthy pagan crew," as they were generally called in those days, but from whom we yet inherit some of the noblest traits of our national life.

That a monk should be chosen for my hero was inevitable, for none but monks would do the work; and if we fairly put in contrast these monks and the heathen among whom they laboured, we shall see this most clearly. I cannot do better than quote here a few words from the late Rev. Charles Kingsley, for although I have placed my story a century later than he names, the exceptional circumstances of England at that time, and the work of the monks among its lawless invaders, make his words equally applicable.

He says:—"The more one studies the facts, the less one is inclined to ask, 'Why was not the work done better?' the more inclined to ask, 'Could it have been done better?' Were not the monks from the fifth to the eighth century exceptional agents, fitted for an exceptional time, and set to do a work which, in the then state of the European

PREFACE

races, none else could have done? At least so one suspects after experience of their chronicles and legends, sufficient to make one thoroughly detest the evil which was in their system, but sufficient also to make one thoroughly love themselves."

Of one or two of these legends I have availed myself in this story. The historical data can be fully verified by consulting any authentic history of the times. The ignorance, superstition, and credulity which my story unfolds are by no means exaggerated, and yet, with all their faults and failings, we must say of these monks, "Wisdom is justified of her children."[1] The mistake made was, that they did not know when their work was done, and that the world had ceased to heed them ages before they ceased to exert their power even in England. But that they have had their uses, that they have done noble work for God and mankind, all must admit, and we may still learn many a useful lesson from the self-denying, devoted lives of monks, who could neither read nor write, yet set themselves steadily to overcome every difficulty in the way of their becoming the greatest and grandest teachers the world has ever seen.

Emma Leslie

[1] LUKE 7:35

HISTORICAL NOTES

From A.D. 793-1066, England was frequently attacked by the Danish Vikings. Although some Vikings came only to pillage the riches of the monasteries, many stayed, settling with their families and building villages.

Several important historical figures are mentioned in *The Martyr's Victory* and although some of them do not play a large role in the story, an understanding of who they were can help to put the story into its historical context. Here is a brief summary of these people:

King Edmund: Edmund became king of East Anglia in eastern England in A.D. 855 at the age of 14. While fighting against the Danish invaders in A.D. 869, Edmund was captured. When he refused to renounce his Christian faith, the Danes killed him, earning him the title, Edmund the Martyr.

King Alfred the Great: Alfred the Great ruled the kingdom of Wessex in southern England from A.D. 871-899. He spent most of his reign fighting successfully against Danish invaders. King Alfred encouraged learning and had many passages of the Bible translated into Old English. He also compiled a list of laws that would eventually form the foundation for the English Common Law.

HISTORICAL NOTES

Guthrum: Guthrum reigned over the Danes in eastern England beginning in A.D. 874. Guthrum then attempted to conquer the kingdom of Wessex and was defeated by Alfred the Great in A.D. 878. As part of the terms of his defeat, Guthrum was baptized as a Christian and took the Christian name of Æthelstan.

Cædmon: Cædmon was an English poet who lived in the seventh century A.D. at a monastery in eastern England. Little is know about him other than that he was renowned for his ability to quickly translate the Latin Scriptures into Old English poetry. Only one short poem definitely known to have been written by Cædmon, has survived.

Bede: Venerable Bede, as he is often called, was a monk in the eighth century in eastern England. Bede wrote extensively on history, science and theology, including commentaries on many sections of the Bible. In A.D. 735, shortly before his death, Bede translated the Gospel of John into Old English.

IMPORTANT DATES

A.D.

840 Birth of St. Edmund

855 St. Edmund crowned King of East Anglia

865 Danish Vikings invade East Anglia

869 St. Edmund martyred by the Danes

871 Alfred the Great crowned King of Wessex

878 Guthrum surrenders to Alfred the Great, converts to Christianity and changes his name to Æthelstan

899 Death of Alfred the Great

906 St. Edmund's body moved to Broderickworth

CONTENTS

ILLUSTRATIONS

The Martyr's Victory

The Martyr's Victory

Chapter I

The Ark of Refuge

THE first bright beams of the morning sun rising above the eastern horizon, gilded the thatched roofs of a group of buildings which, partly of stone, partly of wood, but all strongly and securely built, were clustered round a central and more imposing structure, evidently a church.

And now the strong oaken door of the church was suddenly opened, and a group of serge-clad monks came out into the morning sunshine; not to loiter in its bright beams, however, for each hurried to an outbuilding, and shouldering a mattock or spade, hastened to the fields that lay behind the buildings.

These were no lazy drones, as the fruitful fields testified; and many a poor family in the neighbouring town could do the same; for what they would do if the winter was unusually severe or the

SERGE-CLAD: *wearing garments made of a durable fabric*
MATTOCK: *a tool similar to a pickax, but with a flat blade*
DRONES: *those who do mindless, menial work*

Danes came and drove away their cattle and destroyed their crops, they hardly dared to think, if they could not be succoured by the brethren of the monastery.

These incursions of their neighbours of East Anglia were a never-ceasing trouble and embarrassment to the brethren, and at the present time were the subject of a grave consultation, whether or not their house should be abandoned, and the whole brotherhood removed further south, where King Alfred might afford them some protection.

One of the brethren, now carrying his mattock across his shoulder, and ever and anon casting anxious glances across the barren waste that marked the confines of the East Anglian kingdom, seemed to be musing over this question still, although he did not join in the animated discourse of his companions.

At length he was joined by a young monk who had lately come among them. "Dost thou not think it is labour in vain to till the fields of this monastery?" he said, in something of a discontented tone.

"And wherefore?" asked the elder monk sharply.

"Nay, brother Osric, I meant not to provoke thine anger, but thou knowest that for all our digging and hoeing and seed-sowing, it is mighty little reaping we can get, except a few handfuls be snatched in haste, when the alarm is given that the Danes are upon us."

"That is true, my brother; it is now many years

SUCCOURED: *assisted in time of need*
INCURSIONS: *hostile invasions*
CROZIER: *a staff with a crook or cross on the top*

since the brethren gathered in the rye and wheat and barley, and to feed ourselves and our starving townsfolk last winter our Lord Abbot's silver crozier had to be sold," said the monk quietly.

The young monk looked horrified. "I thought the monastery was very rich," he said. "The Danes say ye can grow gold."

His companion smiled. "Yes, we grow gold for them, golden grain which they tear from the fields ere it be fully ripe. What wouldst thou counsel, my brother?" he asked.

"That we should go southward to King Alfred. He is a great and mighty king now, and he will give us a monastery where we can abide in peace, without damage from the filthy pagans."

"And so thou dost counsel our forsaking this goodly house, where we can protect the weak and tend the sick and feed the hungry? But let me ask thee this, What will the poor folk do next winter? What wouldst thou have done if there had been no refuge here?" asked Osric.

The hot blood came into the young man's face for a moment, but he said, rather haughtily, "I am of thane folk; I am not poor."

"True, thy father is a thane," said Osric quietly, "but thou wouldst have been called nidling before many years were over thine head, for they would never have made a man of thee." There was a touch of contempt in the tone in which this was said, and the young monk's face grew crimson.

THANE: *a free man who owes service to an Anglo-Saxon lord, especially military service*

NIDLING: *a coward; a term of extreme disgrace*

The elder saw that he had pained his young companion, and a feeling of compunction stole over him. "Nay, nay, heed not my words, Egbert; we have need of such as thee, I trow, to copy our books, and learn all clerkly arts. For myself, I could never learn to read," and he stretched out his stalwart arms, drew himself up to his full height, and stopping for a moment to look at his gigantic stature reflected in a pool of water, he said, "I may be wrong, Egbert, but it seemeth to me that God must have other work than reading and writing for such as I."

How the lad envied him his splendid strength and gigantic stature! He, weak, pale and delicate, was only allowed to work an hour or two in the fields for his health's sake. What his companion had said was quite true. In his father's great hall, among the roistering house-carles, there was no place for him, for he could not join in their rough sports, and the sight of a battle-axe or two-handed sword always made him shudder.

He had always retreated to his mother's bower when the weather prevented him from rambling in the woods, until at last the bower-maidens laughed, and whispered among themselves, as they glanced at him in the corner poring over his strip of beech board, on which was roughly cut two or three sentences of the Lord's Prayer in the Saxon tongue, or sorting out the herbs and roots he had gathered in the woods.

COMPUNCTION: *remorse*
TROW: *believe or think*
CLERKLY ARTS: *reading and writing*

These were the only occupations possible for one like him, in those times; and instead of looking forward to the future with hope and anticipation, each year as it came filled poor Egbert's heart with a greater dread and fear; for what room was there for him in the world? His father grumbled, groaned, and blustered by turns, which only made the delicate sensitive lad more nervous than ever, and cost his mother many bitter tears.

To see his mother in trouble was a grief to Egbert almost unbearable, and so, to save her the sight of her useless son, and to escape the scornful looks and whispers of the bower-maidens and house-carles, as well as his father's reproachful anger, the lad took to hiding himself in outhouses and dark closets when he could not go to the woods.

The all-perplexing subject of his thoughts was this: How it was God could let him live, when it was clear there was no room for such as he in the world. The world needed fighting-men, the weak ones only robbed these of the bread that was already too scarce. He had been told this again and again, with many oaths to enforce it, when his father was unusually angry; and one day Egbert went forth to the woods, resolving that he would no longer rob those who had a right to all the world could give them. He would live as long as he could on the roots and acorns that he might find, and when these failed he would lie down and die.

ROISTERING: *noisy and unruly*
HOUSE-CARLES: *household men-servants*
BOWER: *a lady's private apartment in a medieval hall*

But before he had walked far, the thought of his mother quite overcame him, and he threw himself upon the ground, while an irrepressible wail of anguish burst from his lips.

The next minute someone touched him on the shoulder, and starting to his feet he saw a monk before him; a stately commanding man he looked, in spite of his dirty ragged serge frock and cowl. Egbert could only stare in blank surprise for a minute or two, for a monk was rarely seen in that neighbourhood.

"Holy father," stammered Egbert, and then he stopped, for the monk had raised his hand, as if in warning.

"Nay, nay, call me not holy father," said the monk quietly, "I am but a sinful man; call me brother Osric, an thou wilt, and tell me thy trouble; it may be I can help thee," he added, in a winning tone.

But the lad shook his head. "There is no help, for there is no room in the world for such as I;" and he lifted his pale face and looked in wonder at the tall stately monk.

Brother Osric looked down upon him pityingly. "The world is a rough, storm-tossed sea," he said; "but hast thou never heard of the Ark that ever rides securely on its rough billows—the refuge God hath provided for the weak—His holy Church?"

Egbert's pale face grew crimson. "My father drove my mother's confessor from the door seven years ago," he said, "just as I began to read. It was because he found me with this," and he drew from his sleeve his treasured beech board. "Since then, I have heard little but what my mother could teach me," he added.

"So thou didst never hear there was a refuge for the weak—a shelter where such as thee may hide from the world's rough storms, and read books, and gather knowledge, and learn wisdom?"

Egbert shook his head. "I have seen the great monastery west of the Watling Street," he said.

"Would'st thou like to come and dwell there?" asked the monk.

Egbert opened his eyes wide at the question. "Who would have me?" he said.

"The Church will have thee, and help and shelter thee," said the monk.

"But—but I am of no use," said Egbert.

"That is nought to the Church; thou art needy, and she offers thee a shelter—a shelter from the scorn of men. Wilt thou accept it, or wilt thou stay in thy father's house, to be called a nidling?"

How the lad's face flushed at that word! It was the embodiment of all that was mean, cowardly and contemptible; and in that age, when brute force was the only recognized pledge of honour and bravery, a gentle timid lad like Egbert lived in continual dread of it. He shivered now as he heard it, and the monk saw the shudder.

"Nay, nay, my son, think not that I call thee nidling, or that our holy Mother Church doth call the weakest of her servants this name of reproach. Thou art no nidling, I trow, but thou art no warrior either, and thou dost know that the world will call thee the one if thou art not the other."

"I—I would come to thy monastery, and gladly be a monk, an the Church could make use of me," said Egbert; "but wherefore should I eat the bread of a better man, as I am of no use in the world?"

"Nay," said Osric, "but the Church can make use of thee, an thou dost love such things as that," and he nodded rather contemptuously at the slips of beech wood in Egbert's hand.

"I cannot read much," said Egbert sadly.

"But thou canst learn to read, and write too, I trow, and that is more than I can do, and when thou hast learned those, canst copy the books in the monastery scriptorium, and illuminate them too. Who knoweth but thou mayest do one worthy of our Alfred himself to receive?" he added encouragingly.

Egbert forgot his trouble for a moment in the joyful anticipation of seeing and being able to read more wonderful books than his own, and he looked so elated that the monk thought it needful to put in a word of caution. "I tell thee this that thou mayest know the gentle goodness of God in providing something for weak hands to do. I say not that such things as reading and writing are quite useless, since our gracious lord Alfred hath recommended all judges and bishops to learn

SCRIPTORIUM: *a room set apart for scribes*
ILLUMINATE: *to decorate with gold, silver or brilliant colors*

these clerkly arts; but I see that the world will never think aught of these. 'Tis spear and battle-axe for the world, but book and pen for the Church."

"Do ye monks do nought but read and write?" asked Egbert timidly.

A look of contemptuous scorn for a moment crossed the face of Osric. "Book and pen for such as me? Nay, nay, my son, a monastery were no place for me; my penance would be harder than I could bear, an it were so. Nay, nay, our God when He gave the Church to be an ark of refuge, knew that men of might and stature might need to seek its shelter, as well as the weak and helpless, and so there is work for all, the strong as well as the weak. Didst thou ever see our fields, my son?" he asked.

"I have heard that they are ever fruitful, and thy crops always plenteous."

"And wherefore dost thou think this is so?" asked Osric. "Who hath made them fertile? It is well-known that nought would grow in these lands until the monks came, and digged, and watered, and drained, working like giants, with spade and mattock, instead of battle-axe and spear, until corn waved where the bittern boomed, and there were goodly barns built of the forest trees, storehouses filled with food, that God's poor might be fed."

"Then thou dost work in the fields?" Egbert ventured to say, at the same time thinking how contemptuously his father's house-carles regarded

PENANCE: *voluntary punishment for sins committed*
BITTERN: *a large bird that lives in marshes*
BOOMED: *the male bittern's call has a loud booming sound*

this employment. *Their* fields were scratched over rather than dug, and their crops were always poor and thin.

"Yes; the brethren work in the fields," said Osric, after a pause, during which he had been looking at the lad attentively, almost reading his thoughts. He sighed as he did so, and yet, after all, was he not, in spite of his boasting tone, half-ashamed of being a farmer monk, instead of a blustering, roistering warrior, always on the lookout for picking a quarrel with either friend or foe, so that it gave opportunity for a sword to be drawn? Both remained silent for a few minutes, until the monk said, "Well, my son, what dost thou think? thou must choose between the world and the Church."

"The world hath nought that I can do, and so I will come with thee, an thou wilt wait until I have bidden my mother and sister farewell."

"That is well-spoken, my son; there is no room in the world for such as thee: I will wait an hour for thee by the old oak yonder, an thou dost not come back I shall know thou art in thy mother's bower, crying with the maidens, and wilt leave thee for a nidling unworthy of our shelter."

"I will meet thee," said Egbert shortly; and he turned homeward at once to tell his mother. But it was not so easy to leave home as he had imagined. There was his favourite dog and other dumb pets, to say nothing of one or two of the house-carles who had been kind to him, and these had to be passed in the great hall, and cost his heart a pang as he thought of leaving them forever.

But this was as nothing to what he felt when, throwing himself at his mother's feet, he sobbed forth, "My mother, I have come to bid thee farewell."

"To bid me farewell!" said the lady, in a little alarm, as she laid her hand on his fair silky hair.

Then he told her of his meeting with the monk, and the proffered protection of the Church, and whispered of his father's anger on account of his weakness, and finally begged that she would let him go. What could the lady say? She loved her son, dearer than life itself, and knew that she should daily and hourly miss the meek gentle lad who was of no use in the world, and yet she could not bid him stay: nay, she felt thankful that a shelter had been offered him from the world's scorn.

So Osric and Egbert went back together to the monastery, and a friendship was formed between them that day that gradually increased as time went on; and it became the rule, that when Egbert went for the morning walk it should always be to the fields, or wherever Osric's work lay.

PROFFERED: *offered*

Chapter II

The Departure

IT was autumn when Egbert entered the monastery, and during the winter he had applied himself with such zeal and such delight to the acquisition of the arts of reading and writing, that now, in the spring of this year 880, he could read any books in Saxon, and had begun to make good progress in Latin; for all the most valuable books, written on parchment, and brought from Rome, were in the Latin tongue.

Now, as they stood for a moment gazing silently into the pool of water, and talking of those arts, and Egbert saw how lightly they were valued by his friend, something of the old feeling stole over him again, and he wished that he too were strong and able to fight, and then, it might be, he would not wish to have the brethren removed to a place of safety.

He said something of this to his friend as they walked on again, by way of excuse for his cowardly suggestion, and then ventured to ask what Osric thought would be the best means of protecting themselves from these enemies.

"There is but one way, I trow," said Osric quietly, "we cannot drive them out of the land: King Alfred himself did not attempt it, for they are kings of the sea, with their long boats and ash shields, and would but return in greater numbers; therefore we must make them our friends, I ween."

"Friends!" uttered Egbert, "a filthy crew of pagans like these Danes of East Anglia our friends!" and the lad drew himself up with something of disdain.

"Nay, but they must be foes or friends, for the land is not large enough for us to live asunder; at least far enough from them—"

"To be safe from their driving off our cattle, stealing our crops, and setting fire to our houses," interrupted Egbert hotly, "and yet thou dost talk of these being our friends!"

"They are our foes now, but if they were our friends we could abide here in peace; and why should they not be? Didst thou ever think, Egbert, that it was for this 'filthy crew of pagans,' as thou dost call them, that Christ died, and hath bid His Church tell them the good news?"

Egbert looked up in astonishment at the speaker. "But, Osric, who could go to these fierce Danes with such a message, even though it be God's message?" he said.

WEEN: *suppose or imagine*

"I would. I will, an our prior will send me. It is of this I would speak now, Egbert. There is to be a full chapter of the brethren this afternoon, and this business of the Danes robbing our monastery is to be talked of, and some plan formed for protecting ourselves from their pillage in future. Many of the brethren are in favour of thy plan, Egbert, leaving this place and going south; but I would fain try another: let us go to these Danes, and teach them to dig and drain and sow the land and reap crops for themselves; and if they do this they will not have time for fighting and stealing, and we may yet teach them to be Christians, like ourselves."

But Egbert shook his head; such a result to him seemed impossible now, and he would fain have tried to persuade his friend to give up all thought of proposing it; but further talk had to be postponed for the present, as the distant field where Osric's work lay had by this time been reached, and it was time for Egbert to return to the monastery and commence his studies.

The gathering of the monks in chapter this afternoon was looked forward to with no small anxiety by several other brethren in the community, for some of the more timid were very anxious to remove from this exposed borderland, and retire to the south; while others, like Osric, maintained that it would be forsaking the post of duty to leave their present home because it was in a dangerous and exposed position.

PRIOR: *head of the monastery*
CHAPTER: *assembly*
FAIN: *rather*

Which of the two parties would have prevailed it is doubtful to decide; but Osric, by his proposal to carry the Gospel to their foes and teach them the arts of peace, made a few of the more timid yet conscientious brethren, feel so utterly ashamed of themselves and their cowardice, that little was heard of the proposal to leave; it rather turned upon the possibility of sending some of the brethren to East Anglia upon the mission Osric had proposed. He himself had volunteered to go, when he made the proposal, and the next question to decide, if the mission was undertaken, was this—Who should go with him?

To the astonishment of all who knew him, Egbert was the next to offer his service for this hazardous undertaking; but the prior at once decided, to the evident relief of Osric, that he could not go—at least not yet.

"Thou wouldst be a care and a hindrance to thy brethren now; but if, after thou hast been here another year, and this mission to the pagans doth succeed, thou art then minded to join thy brethren, I will consider thy request," said the venerable prior in a gentle considerate tone.

Of course Egbert could not but obey, although he felt disappointed; but still his willing mind made others, who were fitted for the service, ashamed of holding back, and very soon six of the most competent brethren had volunteered for the work. A few had offered and been rejected as well as

VENERABLE: *honored due to great age*

Egbert, which somewhat consoled him, although
he almost dreaded the time coming when he
should have to part with Osric. It was nearer than
he had anticipated, for these monks needed little
in the way of preparation, and the next night was
fixed for the departure. There was a solemn gathering of the whole brotherhood in the little wattled church, to commend to God's care and keeping the six missionaries who were about to carry
the good news of salvation to the "filthy pagan
crew" dwelling in East Anglia.

Some had counseled a delay until messengers
could be dispatched to King Alfred, asking that
an ambassador might be sent to the Danish King
Guthrum, who had been baptized, and at least
professed to be a Christian.

But Osric was urgent that they might leave at
once, before the summer was so far advanced that
they could not sow at least a little of the seed they
were to take with them. He hoped to reach the
court of King Guthrum in time for the annual
gathering of the nation, when it was determined
in which direction war should be made; for it was
a Danish custom that in the spring every freeman
should appear at this general assembly, completely armed and ready to go upon any expedition.
At this meeting they examined what causes of
complaint had been received from the neighbouring nations, their power, their riches, the easiness
with which they might be overcome, the amount

WATTLED: *roofed with woven poles supporting straw or other*
plant material

of plunder that might be gained, or the redress of some injury real or fancied.

Now Osric knew the ways of these most unwelcome intruders, and he had finally come to the conclusion that if life could be made more agreeable, they would not be so rashly ready to throw it away, and if they could only be led to see that there were treasures near home, and thus be persuaded to till their own fields, those of Mercia and Wessex might be allowed to flourish in peace. This had been his argument with the brethren.

Thus while one brother among them had been careful to secure some slips of beech wood for writing, and iron styles, which were used for pens, Osric had begged a goodly supply of useful seeds and one or two agricultural tools.

And so, one sweet spring morning, just as the stars were paling before the coming dawn, the little party issued from the church; some with tear-dimmed eyes, for it might be that the missionaries were only going forth to die, and they were the dearest and best beloved of the whole brotherhood who were thus going forth with their lives in their hands.

Half the brethren were to go with them the first mile of their journey, while the rest remained in the church to pray.

Egbert was one of those allowed to go out, but he could say little to his dear friend, the brave leader of this band of missionaries.

REDRESS: *making right*

It had all taken place so quietly, he was so un-
prepared for such a sudden severance of the sweet
friendship that had grown up between himself
and Osric, that the lad was almost stunned.

Truth to tell, Osric felt this separation from his
young companion very keenly, but he carefully
kept down all expressions of grief or regret: but
when the moment of parting came, he tenderly
embraced Egbert, and whispered, "Only a year,
my brother, and I feel as though thou wert in truth
bone of my bone and flesh of my flesh, the younger
son of my mother. Only a year, Egbert, and thou
mayest join us in our new monastery an thou wilt."

"Yes, yes," almost sobbed the young monk in his
grief; and the next minute Osric had gone.

The monks that remained stood for a moment
to watch the departing brethren, and then fell on
their knees to commend them to God once more:
for it was indeed a perilous mission upon which
the brave monks had set out. Only ten years before,
Ingwair and Ubba, the most savage of the Danes
and Vikings, had carried fire and sword throughout the land. They had leveled to the ground the
monasteries of Croyland and Peterborough, Ely
and Huntingdon, and at length burst upon Thetford. King Edmund made a brief stand, but shortly retired to his castle of Framlingham, unwilling
to sacrifice his troops in a useless struggle. But he
was overtaken by his ferocious enemies, and con-
ducted to Ubba's tent.

"Renounce thy faith in the White Christ!" burst forth the angry Dane.

"My faith is dearer to me than my life, and I will never purchase it by offending my God," was the king's reply. Ubba, in a rage, ordered him to be tied to a tree and whipped, but still the martyr-king refused to renounce his faith. Then, still more enraged, his persecutors shot at him, as he stood bound to the tree, and covered his body with their arrows, and at last beheaded him.

Now this was as well-known to Osric and his brave companions as it was that their own monastery had barely escaped destruction about the same time. It was little wonder, then, that as they plodded on over the barren plain or only half-cultivated fields, with their faces towards the rising sun, they should now and then turn round, as if mutely bidding farewell to each landmark as they passed.

At length one of them said, "King Guthrum is a Christian, and it may be he will give us a monastery at once, for I have heard that many goodly houses have been leased to God in this East Anglia by our Saxon forefathers."

"We will hope in God, not in King Guthrum, my brother," said another; "our house not made with hands at least is sure, and if we can teach but one of these pagans to turn from Odin, their idol all-father, to the one true God, their true Father, it will matter little whether we have a

short shrift and a hasty journey, like the blessed
saint King Edmund, or stay awhile to teach them
how to sow their fields, so that they make the best
of both worlds."

"Well, brother Leof, I am for staying awhile,
an it please God to spare me from the pagans' arrows," said the practical Osric, glancing at the precious little sack of seed he carried over his shoulder. They all carried something for the founding
of a new home in the heathen land. One had a par-
cel of beech boards and a small roll of parchment
for writing, two others carried the simple agricultural tools that were necessary, at least to begin
their work, until they could make others, while
the eldest of the party carried their most priceless
and precious treasure of all, a manuscript copy
of Bede's translation of the Gospel of St. John,
and another in Latin. He was himself an erudite
scholar, and had been offered a post of honour in
the Court of King Alfred, but had refused to leave
his monastery for that, although he was one of the
first to follow the lead of Osric in this mission to
East Anglia.

Two others among them could read and write,
and it would be their duty to copy the precious
manuscripts, or portions of them, and also translate them into the Danish language. It would not
be difficult to do this, Osric assured them, for it
was very similar to the Saxon tongue. He could
speak it fluently. How he had learned it he did not

SHORT SHRIFT: *a hurried time of confession before death*
ERUDITE: *learned*

say, and none of the brethren had ever ventured to ask him; for somehow, Osric, although only an ordinary monk, on a level with themselves, and often working harder at the most menial toil than any of them, was looked up to with as much, perhaps more, reverence than the prior himself.

Whether it was his noble carriage and upright, almost haughty, bearing, or whether it was the reserve he had always maintained about his family and life in the world before he joined them, they would have been puzzled to tell; but no one among them, in their most sportive moments during recreation time, ever dared to trench upon the dignity of brother Osric.

They had come forth, each of them laden with something necessary for their work in East Anglia, but their wallets were empty of food, and so at the first village they reached after sunrise they resolved to beg their breakfast. To do this at any of the little huts that spread like a fringe around the vill or hall where the thane lived, the monks knew would be useless, so they went at once to the residence of the lord, for breakfast would be served about this time in the mead-hall.

This castle, like their own monastery, was a collection of irregular buildings nestling round or leaning against the central hall, the whole being enclosed by a strong stockade, within which not only the thane's family, but all the villagers, could take refuge on the approach of an enemy.

TRENCH UPON: *dishonor*
WALLETS: *knapsacks*
MEAD-HALL: *a large hall used for eating and drinking*

Our party of monks were readily admitted within the rude fortification, and soon became the center of the busy scene in the yard. Cooks and servants, carrying huge joints of meat on iron spits from the kitchen to the hall, stopped to ask for news, whether the Danes would come down upon them again this year.

The house-carles, gathered in groups round them, were asking the same question, while the dogs tumbled and growled and barked at each other, until at a signal from the door of the hall the whole noisy company, dogs included, trooped in to breakfast. At the raised end of the spacious hall, where the thane and his family sat, the walls were hung with embroidered tapestry, but at the lower portion, a plain wall-cloth concealed the rough timbers, and higher up were many pieces of armour—shields, bows, cases of arrows, etc. The upper portion was open to admit the light, the roof being supported on pillars, which gave it rather a summer-house look, but this morning made it very pleasant, for the spring sunshine came through the open portion of the wall, and shone down upon the long oaken tables, or boards, that were now laid upon the trestles for breakfast. For the tables were taken down when not in use, leaving the hall clear for dancing or sports, or a large gathering of people.

Twisted ale-cups and vases, ladles and spoons, were laid on the tables, and just as our friends

VASES: *cups*

entered at the lower end of the hall, came the thane, in his long blue tunic, reaching from his throat to his knees. He gave his uninvited guests a warm welcome, and bade them sit at the upper end of the table; but he did not ask them any questions, for the servants were waiting with the meat on the spits, and everybody was hungry.

Ale and mead were brought in small buckets, and the vases on the tables filled from them, and the drinking went on as vigorously as the eating had done, while the dogs under the tables devoured the pieces thrown down, or picked the bones after their masters had done with them. There were costly gold and silver cups on the upper table, and beautifully formed vases, but a single knife served the need of the family, and there was not a plate among the whole company. Servants on their knees presented lumps of meat on the end of a spit, from which a piece was cut by each person, and held in his fingers until it was all eaten.

The monks had finished their breakfast before anyone else, and so had time to glance at the family table—the thane and his wife, three sons and two daughters.

One of the lads reminded Osric of his young friend Egbert, but he soon noticed that the elder girl glanced frequently in their direction, and he forgot the lad in the interest of looking at her and her beautiful sister, wondering what the future had in store for her, and whether Egbert's sisters were like these two girls, and whether these knew anything of the "good news" they were about to carry to the Danes; for he had noticed that there was no church among the group of buildings clustering round the hall.

Chapter III

The Journey

AS soon as breakfast was over, the thane and his wife went out to the door, where there was already a crowd of beggars collected, and here, assisted by her bower-maidens, who held the basket and handed the bread to her, she earned her right to the title of lady loaf-giver. This duty over, they turned to inquire after their guests, and when all their questions had been answered, brother Dunstan proposed that the servants should be gathered in the hall, that he might conduct a service of prayer and praise to God.

Osric noticed that the girl who had glanced at them so often during breakfast-time turned beseechingly towards her father, as though mutely pleading for the monks' request to be granted, while the lady whispered a word in his ear before he replied. But for this persuasion he would probably have said that his house-carles could not be spared from their work; but to please his wife he soon had them gathered in the hall again, and the old monk, drawing forth his precious manuscript of St. John's Gospel, read part of the third chapter.

In many Saxon households like this a chaplain was kept, and a little church provided for the worship of God; but it was not so here.

When Osric spoke of this to the lady, after the conclusion of the service, she sighed as she said, "Alas, holy father, what can we do, with the Danes continually harassing us? I have asked my husband to build a church, but he says he must strengthen the stockades first, and 'tis useless to ask a chaplain to live among us, when we can barely keep our poor gleeman."

Osric might have urged that a chaplain who could read and teach her children and the servants their duty towards God, as well as their master, would be of more use than a gleeman, whose sole occupation was to sing, and amuse the guests, and feed the family vanity by his recitative accounts of their valour, their riches, or their beauty; but he knew that it would be worse than useless to say this to a Saxon, and so, with a promise readily given that a church should be built, and a man of God engaged to instruct the household, if the Danes could be persuaded to leave them alone, the monks took their departure, resolving to reach the confines of East Anglia by nightfall. Their wallets had been well-filled with bread and meat by their friendly hosts, so that they could eat their dinner as they walked, and they determined to ask any chance traveler they might meet where King Guthrum held his court. They hoped they should not have to travel so far as Thetford, for that would involve another day's march, and through the midst of their foes, who might possibly resent their coming among them, and hinder, if they did not altogether prevent, their reaching the king.

When therefore they heard, late in the afternoon, that the national assembly of freemen was now gathered at Thetford, and that another day's journey was before them, they resolved to pass the night in the shelter of the forest rather than seek it among the Danes, until they knew something of the temper of the people just now.

It was of little moment to these men that they were hungry, and that their few ragged clothes would ill-protect them from the chilling east wind that now blew across the almost desert land. What was cold and nakedness to them, when on such an errand as this? So they raised their voices in concert, at the usual vesper hour, and sang the appointed psalms, and prayed, comforted with the thought that at this hour of sunset their brethren would be lifting their hearts to God likewise, and doubtless on their behalf.

This service of prayer and praise was a strength and refreshment to the weary monks, and at its close the ever practical Osric suggested that two or three of them should go in search of some of last year's acorns, that might have escaped the pigs

MOMENT: *importance*
VESPER HOUR: *time of evening prayers*

or wild boars, for a few of these would be better than nothing, and give them strength for the next day's journey.

So the oldest brother, Dunstan, was left in charge of their few possessions, while the rest went to look for their evening meal. After a diligent search, about a handful was collected and divided amongst them, and then, another psalm having been sung, and prayer offered, they lay down to sleep on the ground, trying to forget that they were in the forest, and reminding themselves and each other that God had promised to protect His servants when engaged in His service.

On awaking the next morning, their first duty was to raise a psalm of thanksgiving to God, and after again commending themselves in prayer to His keeping, they set forward on their journey. They walked on in silence, for they knew by experience that they should feel the gnawings of hunger less if they talked little; and moreover it was safer in this forest, they thought, to be silent, for enemies, human and superhuman, might be lying in wait for unwary travelers in such a place as this. They would have avoided it if they could, as the mightiest warriors often did, or if compelled to pass through it, took care to arm themselves *cap-à-pie* before commencing the journey, lest some more-than-half-savage band of robbers should fall upon and literally devour them.

CAP-À-PIE: *from head to toe*

Then, worse than all to these simple ignorant monks, were the superhuman enemies that were supposed to infest the forests. We can afford to laugh at werewolves and elf-maidens and witch-wives, but they were very real in the belief of all in those days, and might tempt men, not only to danger, but to sin, if they knew they were about to preach the Gospel to those whom Satan still held in his power.

So it was with beating hearts, and ears strained to catch the slightest sound that differed from the whisperings of the breeze that sighed among the budding trees, and eyes that peered and glanced in every direction, lest an enemy should pounce upon them unawares, that these early missionaries pressed through the dread forest, often whispering a word of prayer, and now and then venturing to lift their voices feebly in a psalm, which might help to cheer their sinking spirits.

They made a meal of a few acorns and young leaves, and while sitting down to eat this, the precious manuscript was brought out, and some cheering words of the Gospel read, and then they went on again, refreshed in body and soul, and hoping to be beyond the forest and within sight of Thetford by nightfall.

It needed no words to tell them when they were drawing near to the end of their journey, for the clanging of armour and the shouts of the soldiers warned them that they were close to a camp of the

Danes before they were out of the forest; and pausing now for their vesper service, they heard amid
the murmured petitions of their prayers the names
of Thor and Odin shouted close at hand; and they
wondered whether this service would be their last,
and whether they would be marched straight to
death or allowed to see King Guthrum.

This question was not for them to answer; their
duty was to finish the service appointed for this
hour; and so, the prayer being ended, the singing began. The next moment, a band of warriors,
fierce, but evidently frightened by the strange
sounds, rushed into the presence of the monks.

One or two voices faltered at the sight of the
well-known, much-dreaded Danes, but Osric saw
the fright of the soldiers, and kept up the singing,
and when that psalm was concluded, he began
the twenty-fourth, chanting in a loud triumphant
voice, "The earth is the Lord's and the fullness
thereof, the world and they that dwell therein,"
each verse concluding with a glad shout of, "Hallelujah, Hallelujah, Hallelujah!"

At a signal from Osric, the brethren marched
forward as they sang, and the soldiers fell back, as
they advanced with Osric at their head chanting
their triumphant hymn.

Who were they? Where did they come from?
were questions that the soldiers asked, but did
not wait to have answered; for as the Hallelujah
once more resounded through the forest glades

they beat a hasty retreat, to tell their companions in the camp of the strange visitors who were approaching—whether human or superhuman they could hardly tell, only that a great fear had fallen upon them, as they glided out of the heart of the forest, singing an unknown song in an unknown tongue. This was the story carried to the camp, and meanwhile Osric and his companions had followed, still singing their triumphant Hallelujah.

So East Anglia was entered, as though these servants of God were already conquerors, and had won the land for Him. Osric saw that the Danes knew not what to make of this sudden visit, and drawing himself up to his full height, and assuming a tone of command, he stepped forward a pace or two from his companions, and said, "We are messengers from the King of kings and Lord of lords, to your king, Guthrum, and ye Dane-folk and freemen."

The Danes looked from one to another, for the stranger spoke their own tongue as plainly as they could, and he was evidently not at all afraid of them, which was altogether so strange, so different from what they had seen when a monk happened to fall in their way, that after a few moments' conference among themselves, it was agreed that it would be best to let the strangers pass without molestation, and a messenger was dispatched to the town, about half a mile off, to apprise the king of the visitors that might shortly be expected in

APPRISE: *inform*

Thetford, and the strange manner of their coming.

A strange tale never loses anything of the marvelous in passing from mouth to mouth, and so by the time King Guthrum heard of the coming of his strange visitors, the manner of their arrival was nothing short of miraculous. They had come out of the gloaming, out of the treetops, out of the clouds, so the tale had gathered, until as it was repeated to the king, he almost shook with terror at the thought of these terrible spirits who had assumed the form of Christian monks, and doubtless came by command of the great God in whose name he had been baptized and received his kingdom.

All too well did he know the import of the coming of these messengers; for had he not, in fear of his turbulent people, replaced the gold images of Odin and Thor in the temple from which he had dethroned them, vowing to restore it to its original use as a church? This, and the all but forgotten baptismal vow, returned to his memory, and it was with more terror than patience that he awaited the coming of his supernal visitors.

But the twilight deepened into darkness, and hour after hour passed, each one increasing the fright of the king; for to his anxious inquiries he now heard that nothing had been seen of the six monks since they entered the town. For a moment this had given him relief, until he reflected that

GLOAMING: *dusk*
IMPORT: *meaning*
SUPERNAL: *heavenly*

they would surely come again, come perhaps in the night, and carry him off bodily while he was asleep. No mere mortal, had he been ever so terrible in his might and cruelty, could have inspired the brave Danish king with such fear as now possessed him. It haunted him alike waking or sleeping—nay, he could not sleep; and as he tossed restlessly about on the pile of wolfskins that formed his bed, he trembled at every passing breeze as it sobbed and whistled through the crannies of his rough timber palace. Then he would spring up, and seize his well-covered shield and battle-axe, that always lay by his side, as if to defend himself from some invisible enemy, until he remembered that these were no human foes with whom he could do mortal combat, and what their power might be he could well-imagine, but could not fully know.

He recalled all the wonderful stories he had heard while staying at the court of King Alfred about the power and might of God, and how terrible was His vengeance against those who dared to offend Him. True, he had been told that this great power was far oftener exerted on behalf of men for their good, for the saving of their souls rather than for their destruction; but then he had so fully merited this wrath, that how could he hope to escape the vengeance?

Secure in the heart of his kingdom, and in the terror which his freemen had inspired among all the neighbouring nations, he had dared to forget all about his baptism and the promises he had made then—that he and his people would renounce the worship of idols, and henceforth worship the only living God. His league with the mighty Christian king had been broken too in many particulars, and even now he was meditating a total rupture of the terms by which he held his kingdom; for, urged on by his freemen, gathered from among the North-folk and South-folk, he had almost consented to lead them again into the kingdom of Mercia, for they had grown tired of such simple predatory warfare as burning a few houses, driving off all the cattle they could find, and destroying the growing crops.

True, they had carefully searched for some cause of quarrel they could bring against Mercia; but even the national assembly had been obliged to confess that they could find nothing; neither did their careful looking into their neighbours' affairs, who lived on the borderland, offer them any hope of gain, for they had so impoverished them time after time that there was nothing left that they could take. Of course it had not been pleasant to declare all this to his loyal freemen, who had come to this great gathering ready armed and impatient to set out on some warlike expedition.

Each year brought some young men with white unscarred shields, but they had seldom returned home with them undented, and the more marks they could show of the warfare, the prouder were the possessors; for this was a Dane's glory, above all others, to have a well-worn, well-battered shield.

But for the last year or two there had been no chance of winning this glory, and Guthrum, as he looked at the number of unblemished shields, knew not what he should do to pacify his restless subjects unless he consented to lead them forth to battle and victory somewhere. It did not matter much to the warriors where they went, so that they could win glory and plunder; and the invasion of Mercia was now the subject under consideration, and Guthrum had at last resolved to yield to the demands of the people, since he could not safely withstand them. Could it be that God, knowing his thoughts, as the monks said He did, had sent His messengers charged with the full powers of vengeance to be wreaked upon him, if he dared to carry out the proposal that had been laid before him? It was a question that puzzled the king sorely, but the more he thought of it, the more convinced he became that this was the special object of their visit, else why should they come at such a critical time? They had descended from the clouds, the messengers said, and, it seemed, must have gone up there again, after viewing the camp; but they would doubtless come to him in the morning, and how should he meet these messengers of God?

Chapter IV

At the Court of the Danish King

WHILE the Danish king was torturing himself with fears and anxieties about his
strange visitors and their non-appearance at his
palace, they were scarcely less frightened than he
that they had been prevented from following the
messenger sent to announce their arrival; but just
before entering the town, father Dunstan, the oldest of the party, suddenly fell down fainting.

Some of the monks were greatly alarmed, and
saw in this a warning of coming evil, but Osric said
quietly, "Nay, nay, it is but faintness from want of
food, and the singing our Hallelujah hath taken
all his strength away. Let us carry him aside; I see
a little copse yonder, and it may be we shall find
some water near."

The whole party were so weary and exhausted
with their long march and want of food, that it
was as much as they could do to carry their companion to the little grove of trees; but Osric was
so anxious that it should be done before any of

COPSE: *wooded area*

the heathen saw them, that when they succeeded at last in getting him there, two others were quite incapable of moving further, and lay on the grass almost as helpless as father Dunstan himself.

Osric began to fear that their last effort would cost them dearly, for he knew not where to get food except by begging it of the Danes, and that he felt most unwilling to do just now, for he could see that they were regarded as something more than ordinary monks, and he intended to take advantage of this if possible. He knew these heathen better than his companions, and was perfectly aware that if the impression they had made upon the soldiers was to be maintained, they must not see them thus fainting from exhaustion and hunger, for there was nothing these Danes despised like weakness.

So Osric carefully looked round before venturing from the little sheltered nook where his companions lay, and after watching for some time he espied a poor old woman, who he felt sure was a captive. He beckoned her towards him, and spoke in the Saxon tongue, saying they were messengers from the great God, the All-Father, to King Guthrum, but that they needed food after their long journey through the forest. The sight of a Christian monk, and the sound of her own language, so overcame the poor old creature, that she burst into tears of joy, and eagerly offered to get them what they wanted, and as readily promised to keep their secret. But by the time the food was brought and eaten it was so late, that they decided to postpone their visit to the king until the next day.

The palace of Thetford was little more than a huge barn, made strongly of timbers, in much the same fashion as the house of a Saxon thane, for it had been built by the Angles before the Danes came, and was the residence of King Edmund just before his martyrdom.

But although the outside was rough and grim in its appearance, the inner walls were hung with spoil and plunder torn from many a mead-hall of Mercia and Wessex. No plain common wall-riff hung here, but the whole of the space was covered with rich embroidery, the work of many noble Saxon ladies, who had seen husband and father murdered when this was stolen: jeweled cups and vases, armour, battle-axes, costly bracelets, and even a bishop's robe, miter, and silver crozier, were suspended from wooden pegs, which had been driven through the embroidered arras, regardless of spoiling it. The monks as they entered saw the silver crozier and miter, and it stirred their hearts with indignation to see them thus exposed as trophies in the palace of this pagan king. But the anger they felt about the crozier was as nothing to that which flashed from their eyes as, advancing into the hall, they saw the king drinking wine from one of the sacramental cups which must have been carried off from some church.

WALL-RIFF: *wall decorations, literally "wall rubbish"*
MITER: *tall, pointed hat*
ARRAS: *tapestry*

At the sight of this desecration of a sacred vessel, Osric forgot all prudence—all he had intended to say in his address to the king, and raising his arm, he thundered forth, "Hold, Guthrum, King of the Danes, and pollute not that sacred vessel with thy lips!"

Dunstan and the rest of his companions trembled with fear as they heard this rash speech; but, to their intense surprise, instead of resenting it, the king almost dropped the cup, and instantly pouring out the wine among the rushes on the floor, he held it towards Osric saying, "What more will ye have? From whence come ye? Who are ye?" but it was asked with paling lips, and Osric detected the terror that lay under the assumed light words.

"We are the messengers of the great God, the All-Father whom King Guthrum vowed to serve," answered Osric firmly.

The tall commanding form of the monk, standing erect in the center of the hall, and pointing upwards as he spoke, might well command the respect of even this Danish king and conqueror, without the adventitious aids of superstitious fears. But these entered so largely into the king's conception of the power of the unknown strangers, that he who had never quailed before mortal man fairly trembled now, for he knew that he was guilty of slighting and forsaking the service of this mighty God, and doubtless these messengers knew it too.

SACRAMENTAL: *communion*
ADVENTITIOUS: *added*

And so, despite the presence of his stout war-riors and sturdy house-carles, Guthrum began excusing himself for lapsing into idolatry, and setting up the images of his gods again in the church that had at first been used for the service of God.

Osric did not interrupt the king's speech by a single word, but his eyes flashed and kindled as he listened to the story of how Thor and Odin had been set up again.

"The Danes know not the God of the Saxons; Odin and Thor are the mighty—"

"Nay, but the God of the Saxons is the God of all the earth," interrupted Osric, as after a slight pause the king began speaking again; "He is King of kings, and Lord of lords, and thou hast done despite to Him, and to His saints, and therefore I am come to—"

"Nay, nay, come not with vengeance and anger," interrupted Guthrum, suddenly remembering the miraculous appearing of his visitors, and never doubting but that Osric might the next moment, like their own Thunderer, hurl forth destruction upon them all; for there was no knowing what se-cret power, magical or otherwise, they might not possess.

"Dane, didst thou not promise to hate what thou hadst adored, and adore what thou hadst hated? What of thy troth plighted, too, to King Alfred?" Osric demanded.

DONE DESPITE: *insulted*
TROTH PLIGHTED: *loyalty promised*

As he asked this latter question the king trembled more than ever, for this confirmed all his fears concerning the spiritual or magical power of these visitors, for how else could they know that he was about to violate the treaty by invading Mercia? and he said, "I will not forget the promise I have given to King Alfred; my freemen shall go back with their white shields, and the land of Mercia shall no more be troubled. Speak for me to thy God, great messenger, and tell Him that Guthrum the Dane doth put hands in His, and will be His man."

"But the Lord God is righteous, and hateth those who keep not covenant, who rob and despoil monasteries and churches, and homes where little children and helpless women dwell. Ye are guilty of the seven deadly sins, and would now add to these last the plunder and pillage of the peaceful land of Mercia, robbing the helpless, the fatherless and the widow, whom God would have all men defend."

Osric had no intention of preaching a sermon when he began, but seeing how things were by what the king had said, he forgot all personal danger in the absorbing thought that he would save Mercia from this threatened scourge, if it was possible; and so with words of burning eloquence he threatened the Divine vengeance if this project was not given up at once, not only by the king but by the soldiers too.

It was well perhaps, both for Osric and the king, that most of the leaders, the generals of the wild Danish warriors now encamped outside the town, were at this time present and heard the strange visitor's sermon. He did not spare them, although his companions trembled with apprehension when they heard him flatly accuse them of murder, sacrilege, theft, cruelty, and all the sins that go to make up the black catalogue of a half-wild heathen's life. But they knew that what Osric said of them was perfectly true, though how he should know so much about it was a puzzle not to be accounted for, except by the miraculous appearance of their visitors, which placed them at once above and beyond mere mortal men.

Had they not been such blind slaves to their belief in the marvelous and the magical, the monks' lives would hardly have been worth an hour's purchase, and Osric knew this. Now, however, there was little to fear, if only he could hide the terror of his companions; and so, after concluding his sermon with an offer of pardon if the king and all who were with him would turn from the evil of their ways and repent, he said to Guthrum, "Command thy servants that they lead us to the church, and remove from thence the filthy idols with which it is defiled;" and taking the silver crozier from its peg in the wall as he passed, he led them out, closely followed by some of the servants, whom the king had ordered to do the monk's bidding.

SACRILEGE: *stealing from God*

The golden images of the Danish gods were quickly removed, and when every vestige of the old heathen worship was turned out, the brethren held a service of prayer and praise, to rededicate the little wattled church to the worship of God.

Then Osric sent to demand the sacred vessels he had seen on King Guthrum's table, and placed them on the altar before the holy rood; and once more the bell sounded, calling the people to the house of God; and when at length a few came in, shyly and timidly, father Dunstan stood up and told them they had come to teach them the Christian faith, the good news that God loved all men, and took especial care of the weak whom others despised, and would watch as a wolf against those who cruelly oppressed the poor and needy.

King Guthrum hardly knew what to do when he heard the church bell ring once more. He recalled some of the miracles he had heard of from the monks while staying at King Alfred's court, and wondered whether some of these were to be reacted here in Thetford.

It certainly was not unlikely, if what he had heard was true concerning the martyr King Edmund, whom his countrymen had killed ten years before, not destroying him as they supposed, but exalting him to a kingdom greater than East Anglia, or even all England, and procuring to themselves a foe far more powerful than King Alfred. Doubtless, if these men were monks, as many began to

VESTIGE: *trace*
ROOD: *a large crucifix*

think, it would not be safe to speak them other than fair, since they were in league with the saint whom the Danes had every reason to be afraid of. They might propitiate him not merely to let them alone, but to forgive his cruel death, and by and by he might so far forget it as to show them some favour, and give prosperity again to his earthly kingdom, which since his death had become little better than a waste howling wilderness overrun by men little less savage than the wolves and boars of the forests, and almost as hard to rule, as King Guthrum knew to his cost.

Now, if he spoke these monks fair, and did his best, as became a Danish chief and a king, to the saint himself, surely he would so far forget that deadly flight of Danish arrows as to help him to govern his turbulent subjects, if he promised for himself and for them to become Christians and learn the ways and manners of Christian nations. And if these strangers were but mortal men, as the Danes had begun to find out they were, they were certainly not like themselves, but men whom the gods were likely to inspire and make their messengers.

A man, pure, calm, just, and brave, like this Osric, was little less than a saint here on earth as compared to themselves—a fitting messenger of the White Christ—the God-man in Whose name he had been baptized. They were wise too, these monks; some of them could read and write and

PROPITIATE: *make peace with; regain an offended person's favor* cipher, and knew strange learning about the stars in the heavens and the nature of plants and roots, and how to coax even barren soil to yield them plentiful crops. Why, surely, the very coming of these men boded favour from the saint, for they had been several days in Thetford now, and no disaster had followed—nay, the turbulent assembly of armed freemen had begun to disperse, and the men were returning homewards, disappointed, it is true, at only having white shields to carry back again, but he doubtless owed it to the coming of the monks that they were not now in rebellion, since he had refused to lead them against Mercia.

These were some of King Guthrum's more matured and sober thoughts about the coming of the strange visitors, and having made up his mind to ask them to stay, now they had come, he presented himself in church one day and some of his warriors with him. When the service was over he waited to see the monks, and as Osric was the spokesman of the party always, he addressed himself to him.

"Since God and the White Christ will have me to be His man, I must even ask ye, His messengers, to stay and teach me and my people how to serve Him; and as we are verily guilty concerning your saint-king Edmund, and would fain beseech him to pardon us and grant us his favour, that the land may again be rich and prosperous, I will give you as much land as ye can enclose within a day's march, wherein ye may build a house to dwell in and a church for the worship of God; and moreover I will bid my people come to do whatsoever thou mayest bid them in the work of building. And when the church is built, thou shalt baptize them, as I and some of my chief officers were baptized."

Osric listened in silence to all the king said, striving to hide the joy he felt, for they had begun to fear, from the king's long silence and nonappearance at church, that they should presently be driven out of the kingdom, and the idols once more enthroned on God's altar. He could hardly resist bursting forth into a psalm of thanksgiving when he heard the king's generous offer, but he dared not show all he felt, and he was thankful that his companions did not understand enough of the Danish language yet to comprehend all that the king had said, or they would certainly have betrayed something of the joy this would give them.

Bowing his head with calm dignity as the king finished his speech, he said, "Doubtless the blessed saint-king is favourably disposed to this his sorrowful land, and I will pray the great God to show us what His will is concerning this matter whereof thou hast spoken, and where He will that we choose the land that thou dost promise to give us."

Osric said this, that Guthrum might know they were not to be cheated into occupying a swamp, where only bitterns and frogs could live, or a sandy waste that would not repay them for cultivation; and it was to consider this matter, and consult with his brethren, that he declined to give an answer to the proposal until the third day from then.

The king was evidently a little disappointed that Osric showed no more gratitude; but if he had waited a few minutes outside the church, he would have heard such a song of rapturous praise ascending to God, that he would not have doubted whether the monks *felt* grateful.

Chapter V

The Fugitive

AFTER calmly considering the offer of King Guthrum, and the very different reception they had met with from that which they had feared, brother Leof exclaimed, "They know not we are mere simple monks, or we should be sent packing from Thetford, I trow."

"Simple monks? We are messengers from the great God, sent to proclaim His message of peace and goodwill to men, even this filthy pagan crew," said another.

"Most true, brother; and since we are His messengers, it behooveth us to see to it that we are faithful and true to the trust committed to us," said Osric.

"Nay, but dost thou think we shall fall to worshiping Odin, as the king hath, just to please these pagans?" said Leof in a half-offended tone.

"Nay, brother, I spoke but of myself. Each doth know the weakness of his own heart better than doth his brethren. And now, father Dunstan, what dost thou propose we do in the matter of this offer from the king?"

"Thou wilt not leave Thetford and this church, since the king doth desire us to stay," said the elder monk.

"We may not all abide in Thetford, for Thetford is not East Anglia; but it were well for thee and brother Leof to abide here, I trow; and when he is able to speak this Danish tongue more perfectly we will journey to the South-folk of this kingdom of East Anglia, and there make choice of such land as may be fit, whereon we can build a goodly abbey and plant fields, and teach the people and all who may come to us."

This proposition of Osric's did not find universal favour among the brethren. They were willing to stay at Thetford, where everything promised so fairly for the future, but to go forth into the wilderness again, and risk being received with contempt and scorn, perhaps violence, by these South-folk, was simply folly. Better stay where they were, and make the most of the impression they had already made in the minds of the Danes, counseled two or three.

"Nay, nay, but thou dost forget, my brother, we came here as messengers," said Osric. "Will these pagans think aught of us, or of our message, think ye, if we are content to live easily upon what the king may give us here? Two can preach and teach all who will hear them in this town, as well as six, and we who are strong will go forth again, and make a home, it may be in the wilderness, that shall be a refuge for the weak and a school for those who desire to learn; and thou mayest do the same here, for I doubt not the king will give ye a house to dwell in, and a piece of land where ye may sow and reap. We will divide the seed we brought with us, and it may be that next year we may eat of the fruit sown in this goodly land, for it is a goodly land, albeit the pagans have it in possession."

Having settled the matter thus with the brethren, Osric now had to propose the same terms to King Guthrum—that he would accept a small piece of the offered land here, and the rest in some other place; but to his surprise he met with some opposition to this proposal. The king would fain have detained Osric in Thetford, if all the rest had departed, and he promised to give not only the church, and a house near his own palace, but land to build an abbey near the town, if he would only stay.

But Osric was firm in his refusal. "I am but a messenger, and must go whither I am sent, and it was not to help thee rule this people that the great All-Father sent me hither, but to the people themselves, to teach them that there is other work for them to do in the world than fighting and plundering their neighbours; and this message I must bear to the South-folk, to tell them that God and their blessed saint-king Edmund hath a favour towards them: and then will I claim the land thou hast promised to give us."

King Guthrum was well-pleased to hear that the martyred king bore no ill-will to the Danes for depriving him of his earthly kingdom, but still he did not want Osric to leave Thetford just yet.

"If it will please the saint-king to let thee, his messenger, abide awhile here among the North-folk, to teach them all clerkly arts and learning, thou shalt choose the best of the land to build thee an abbey and a church."

"Nay, but wouldst thou give Saint Edmund less than the best—of his own land too; for knowest thou not that he is in heaven King of East Anglia, and in that thou hast been baptized doth suffer thee to rule over it?"

"The king-saint shall have of the best to be his own again, and I would fain make league with him through thee his messenger, and promise that if he deal fairly with me and my freemen, I will ever protect the abbeys and holy houses that may be built among us."

"Be sure the blessed Saint Edmund will be faithful to his country. And now, an it please thee, I will choose the land, that our brethren may sow and reap of their own, and be not burdensome to thy people; I would fain see the fields digged, and an abbey built, before I go forth from Thetford."

The king was willing enough to give them the land, since Osric would be detained to see to the

SUFFER: *allow*

digging and building, and this work was commenced the very next day.

To the Danes, who knew nothing of agriculture, but lived by plunder, it was a most curious sight to see these monks turning up the soil with their spades and mattocks, and afterwards putting in the seed.

The king had lent the help of some of his slaves to drive stakes into the ground to keep out the cattle, and fell the trees to build the abbey. At length everything was set in order at Thetford, and Leof had learned something of the Danish tongue, and Dunstan was convinced at last that it was the best thing that could be done, although he felt sad at being left behind among the Danes with only Leof to bear him company. But Osric declared they had already lingered too long, for the summer was passing, and another abbey must be built before the winter came.

Then, laden with presents from King Guthrum, and promising to come again within a year and a day, and see how it fared with them at Thetford, and tell what progress he had made among the South-folk, he and his three companions turned their faces once more towards the forest, now in full leaf.

They went as they came, singing psalms of thanksgiving to God, and praying Him to guide them to a suitable spot where they might raise the minster and become a blessing to the people round.

MINSTER: *church*

Many a weary mile was traversed, through forests, and across bare plains cleared by the great fires that had scorched and blackened all the earth for miles round; but nearly a week passed, and as yet no place was found suitable for their purpose. It was summertime, and so they were not at such a loss for food as when they first came. They lived on roots and berries, caught a few trout in the streams now and then, and cooked them at a fire of sticks; and but for their continued fear of falling in with enemies, natural or supernatural, might have enjoyed their pleasant quest wandering through the woodland glades.

At length, after six days' wandering up and down, they met a man searching for some swine he had lost, and after telling him in which direction he would find the animals, Osric asked him if he could tell him where he should find some goodly land, cleared ready for planting and building, yet close to the forest, where they might cut timber, and near to a running stream, that they might have water at hand.

They had not yet found a spot answering all these requirements, and the others, in their impatience, had been willing to forego one or other of them, but not Osric. "God will guide our feet to a place worthy of being set apart to His use," he said, and so they had kept on their way.

The swineherd looked curiously at the monks, but at length he said, "There is the Ea, it hath two goodly streams and plenty of forest land, besides pasture for the cattle."

So to the Ea, or island, they bent their steps, wondering not a little what kind of reception they would meet with among these South-folk—whether they had heard anything of their arrival at Thetford from the freemen, who had certainly been there, and would as certainly bring back the news of their coming.

Before they had got out of the forest, however, they were startled to see a young girl, who was so much afraid of the monks that she instantly darted off in an opposite direction; but a scream was heard at a short distance a minute or two afterwards, and Osric went at once to see what had happened and whether he could help the girl, for he knew it must be she.

He found her lying upon the ground, but trying to crawl away as she heard him approach, and as he drew near she raised her streaming eyes to his, saying, "Kill me an thou wilt, but oh! send me not to Odin, for I am a Christian, and—"

"Nay, nay, fear not, for I too am a Christian;" and then for the first time the girl saw, what she had failed to notice in her terror, that Osric did not wear the short, close-fitting tunic and trousers of her Danish masters, but the garb of a Christian monk.

"Oh save me! save me! save me from being sent to Odin! I feared thou hadst been sent to drag me back to the altar!" and then a deathlike paleness suddenly overspread her agonized face, and she lay helpless at the monk's feet.

For a minute or two he stood looking at her, wondering how he could help her to escape, and as he looked he saw she was an Angle, one of the previous inhabitants of the country before the Danes had it in possession. Those of the Angles not actually killed had been for the most part reduced to slavery, and this girl was one of them, he had no doubt; and now that he came to reflect, it was the sixth day of the sixth month, and therefore a religious festival among the Danes, when sacrifices, both human and animal, were made to Odin. There having been no campaign this spring to supply them with captives for sacrifice, they had been compelled to fall back upon their household slaves to supply the deficiency; and these circumstances rapidly passed through Osric's mind, as he stood looking at the prostrate girl, puzzled to know how he could help her under the existing circumstances.

She was apparently about eighteen, tall and fair, with fine silky hair, which, however, had been cut off to within a few inches of her head, as a badge of her enslaved condition; for only freemen and women were allowed long hair. After standing irresolute for a minute or two, Osric returned to his brethren, and then, while one went in search of water to revive her, the others came to where she

PROSTRATE: *lying flat on the ground*

lay, to try and ascertain whether she was hurt, and if she knew of a place of safety which they could help her to reach. It was some time before she revived sufficiently to be able to speak, and then when she attempted to rise she fell back again, almost screaming with the pain in her foot. On looking at it, Osric, who was a skillful leech, saw that it was very much swollen, and appeared to be dislocated, so that it was quite impossible for her to walk now, even if she had known of a refuge at hand, which she did not.

"I must die in the forest!" said the girl, with a pitiful air of resignation; "that will be better than being sacrificed to Odin, for I can die as a Christian here."

The monks looked blankly at each other in their perplexity, for what could they do in such a strait as this? At length, as if answering the mute question, Osric said, "We can pray," and they all knelt down beside the prostrate girl and prayed that she might be hidden from her enemies and protected in the forest, even though a miracle had to be wrought in her behalf; for the age of miracles was by no means passed away, according to the belief of the monks, and they expected—nay felt confident—that God would send one of His angels to be the girl's special guardian and protector.

But until the angel should arrive Osric wisely determined to make the best use of what means they had at hand for her protection, and so while

LEECH: *physician or surgeon*
STRAIT: *difficulty*

one collected fresh young leaves, and dug a few
roots that were fit for food, another fetched a horn
of water, and placed it within her reach, and Osric
bandaged up her foot with a strip of linen he had
provided himself with before leaving the monastery, in case any of the brethren had met with a
similar accident, and wetting this with some cold
water from the spring, and laying over it some
cool leaves, they left her in a sheltered nook under
the shadow of a great oak. Then they went on in
the direction of the town on the Ea, from which
the girl had just escaped, and near to which was a
bridge of logs laid across the little river.

As they drew near a spacious grove of oak and
ash trees, they heard the sound of riotous feasting
and revelry, and as they came closer to the trees
they saw three of Odin's victims, slaves like the girl
they had left in the wood, hanging dead from the
branches of the trees, while a little beyond, a noisy
crowd was gathered round huge joints of meat that
were roasting on spits before enormous fires—the
animals that had been slain for their blood to be
offered to Odin. These formed the feast that was
to follow, with plenty of ale and mead to wash it
down the giant throats of those who now stood
watching the process of cooking.

The monks had ample time to look at their for-
midable foes from beyond the sacred grove, which
they took good care not to approach too closely,
for the priest was doubtless still in the immediate

neighbourhood, sprinkling the blood of the victims on the stones of the altar or the trees around it. The people had also received their bedewing of blood, as they were gathering round the fires in anticipation of the feast that was to follow, but the priest would still be busy for some time examining the entrails of the animals slaughtered, that they might learn the mind of the gods and how they were disposed to regard them just now.

Their votaries beyond, tall stalwart men, of proud and defiant carriage, ever on the lookout for a quarrel with their friends and neighbours, if they were not provoked by their enemies, were now drinking to Odin and Thor, and clashing their lances against their shields. Many of them were veterans in arms, as could be seen by the insignia of the battles they had fought, which were carved upon their shields; but there were a good many white ones among them, for no man was allowed to decorate his shield with any marks until he had earned this distinction by engaging in battle, and the owners of these white shields looked with envy upon their more fortunate and older companions, and were more ready than any to resent an affront or fancied slight. They were not people to be provoked lightly. Tall, muscular, weather-beaten men, their long fair hair floating like elf-locks in the breeze, they looked the very impersonation of strength and daring, as they moved about with giant strides, or lay stretched

BEDEWING: *sprinkling*
ENTRAILS: *intestines*
VOTARIES: *worshipers*

upon the ground quaffing huge horns of ale and mead, and swearing round oaths about something that seemed to be a universal cause of complaint among them.

At first the monks thought it must be the loss of their destined victim that was the cause of this universal grumbling among them, but on looking towards the sacred grove and its bleeding victims Osric saw that three hung there, the requisite, the sacred number; so being somewhat at a loss to understand what could agitate the assembly at such a festival as this, he bade the brethren stay behind the grove, while he crept a little nearer, that he might hear something of what was going on, and perhaps obtain information that might prove useful by and by.

REQUISITE: *required*

Chapter VI

The Festival of Odin

STRETCHED upon the ground, with horns of ale and mead close at hand, the fair-haired, weather-beaten, ferocious-looking giants were discoursing of the disappointment they had felt at the abandonment of the plan for invading Mercia. Having nothing else to do in the way of fighting this spring, one or two family feuds had been avenged, and there had been more than the usual amount of quarreling among these irascible people and their friends, so that of the inhabitants of the Ea scarcely anyone would speak to his neighbour, and it was only with kindred coming from a distance that they would converse now.

"Look at the white shields that are here! dost thou wonder we are ill-content? 'Tis enough, I say, to make our gods forsake us, for our lances to lie idle and our battle-axes to grow rusty," said one.

His companion shook his head ruefully. "Will Guthrum provide us with cattle and corn to feed our wives and little ones in the winter?" he said.

IRASCIBLE: *irritable*

"Will the new God, whom he hath again vowed to serve, keep us from starving I wonder, if we burn not a few monasteries and carry off their corn and cattle?"

"Yes, He will," boldly answered a voice close at hand; and the next moment the tall form of Osric was seen in the midst of them. Intent upon their talking and drinking, they had not seen him approach until he was there, coming from they knew not whither. One or two reached out their hands and grasped their battle-axes, while others sprung to their feet and waited but a sign from one of the leaders to kill him at once.

But, brave themselves, these Danes could recognize and honour bravery in others; at least just now, when they were comparatively cool. Had it been a little later, when they had had more drink, it might have been different. As it was, a few low growls from their elders caused those who had been ready to seize Osric to drop sullenly into their places again, while he whom the monk had just answered said, "Thou art tired of thy life, I trow, to beard Odin's men without cause."

"Nay, but the White Christ, Whose man I am, hath a controversy with thy gods." Like a war-horse who smells the battle afar off, these warriors roused themselves at the word "controversy," and their blue eyes sparkled with pleasure at the thought of a conflict among the gods. If they might only join in it too, they would gladly do it, asking

BEARD: *challenge*

no payment, but that they might die in the thick
of the fight, and thus be worthy to present themselves in the halls of Valhalla among the heroes
of Odin. In a moment every horn was raised and
filled afresh, and then, amid the clash of arms, the
name of Thor, their mighty war-god, resounded
on every side, and the horns were drained at a single draught.

While the excitement was at its height, a horn
of ale was presented to Osric, while a loud voice
cried, "Let the White Christ's man drink to his
God, for he is bold and brave, and worthy to put
his hands on the mallet of Thor and be his man!"
It was the highest compliment that could be paid
to him, and Osric knew the temper of his auditors
too well to refuse; and so, taking the horn, and
mutely praying for help and strength and guidance, he said aloud, "I drink to the Great God of
all the earth, the All-Father, and His Son the Lord
Christ, who hath died to redeem us." A deafen-
ing shout rang through the woods in response to
this, and then, having shouted again for Odin,
they threw themselves on the ground, and readily
promised to listen to all Osric wished to say about
his God, and the errand that had brought him
into their midst so suddenly and unexpectedly.

"Didst thou not come to Thetford, at the holding of the Al-thing?" asked one.

"Yes, and thy king Æthelstan hath given us land
hereabout, and sent a ring in token of this same
thing."

VALHALLA: *Viking "heaven"–the hall of Odin where warriors who died in battle were received*

"Æthelstan!" repeated one, with a sneer; "dost thou think Guthrum is to be Alfred's man, that thou callest him by this name?"

"Nay, but he is God's man, and hath put away the images of the false gods out of the church at Thetford, and doth command all ye to do likewise; therefore he is right worthy of the noble name given him at his baptism." Several laughed derisively when he spoke of the king's baptism; but they were willing to listen to what Osric said, when he tried to explain something of the Christian faith to them.

As he finished, one of the Danes rose and said, "Now will I tell thee of Odin, the terrible and severe god, the father of slaughter, who giveth victory and reviveth courage in the conflict, who nameth those who are to be slain. In the day-spring of the ages there was neither sea nor shore nor refreshing breezes. There was neither earth below nor heaven above to be distinguished. The sun had then no palace, the stars knew not their dwelling-places, the moon was ignorant of her power and—"

"Nay, nay, we have heard enough," interrupted two of his companions, stopping this recital, "thou art fond of hearing thine own tongue wag, Thordstein."

"Ah, ah, Thordstein is more ready with his tongue than his battle-axe," laughed another. The incautious words had scarcely been uttered before

AUDITORS: *listeners*
AL-THING: *an important Viking gathering*

Thordstein had sprung to his feet, and seizing his armour, challenged his friend to settle the dispute by single combat; and the other, nothing loth, instantly responded, and the two repaired at once to a little distance, followed by all their companions, applauding each of them for their resolution, and rejoicing in this incident, that would give zest to what otherwise seemed rather a tame sort of festival.

Osric knew it would be worse than useless to attempt to interfere between the combatants, and not wishing to partake of the feast, which would shortly be served—the meat having been previously offered to an idol—he took this opportunity of rejoining his companions, who would doubtless soon grow anxious for his safety if he did not return.

In spite of the favourable reception that had been accorded him, he deemed it wiser to keep out of the way for the rest of that day; for when the duel was over there would be sure to be more drinking, and doubtless before the six days' festival came to an end, more than one of these quarrelsome giants would lie cold and dead upon the earth.

So the brethren went back to the edge of the wood, and though they could hear faintly the noisy shouts of the revelers, it did not disturb them; and after the usual evening service, they lay down to sleep under the shelter of the trees.

NOTHING LOTH: *very willing*
REPAIRED: *moved*

Early the next morning they went to see whether the girl they had helped the day before was still in the same hiding-place, to gather some roots for her to eat, and put fresh water within her reach, if she was still unable to move. Osric did not go with them, but went in search of the thane who held command of Ea under the king, and to him delivered the pledge that was sent in token of his being a true messenger, and arranged for the enclosure of the land on which the abbey was to be built.

The thane said they might enclose as much land as they needed, if they would promise to send him a dish of trout from the stream every week, and would also keep some little distance from the sacred grove and altar of their god. This of course Osric was quite willing to do, more especially when the thane agreed that he and his house-carles and lithsmen would willingly listen to him, if he liked to come sometimes and tell them of the ways and doings of the Christians' God, in the mead-hall of his vill.

On his way back he heard that Thordstein had been seriously wounded in the duel, and now lay helpless and almost hopeless, cursing his hard fate that he had not died wielding his battle-axe, instead of lingering on to die at last in his bed, like a rat in its hole, instead of like a hero and a Dane, on the battlefield or in mortal combat.

His wife, who dearly loved her husband, was

LITHSMEN: *mercenary troops from the shipmen's guild*

bowed down with grief that he would not let her do anything to cure his wounds; while at the same time she fully sympathized with his distress at not dying in the fight. Much as she loved him, she would far rather have had him brought home to her dead than hopelessly maimed, so that he could not again go to the field of battle. Her dead hero she might avenge, and glory in his noble death, like many another Danish widow, but now they would only be objects of pitying scorn if he lay there long, to die quietly at last—a fate every Danish hero dreaded. Nay, her very love, strong and tender as it was now, might fail under such a strain as this, for had she not met her former husband when he and his fellow-soldiers were completely routed in the battlefield, and compelled to fly? Had not she, with other wives left in the camp, turned upon the fugitives and driven them back to face the enemy once more? Nor did she repent of this when she found him afterwards among the remnant who had been thus compelled to make that last desperate charge; for had he not died facing the enemy, with his wounds all in front? and when she saw that, she let her grief have its way for a few moments, and then with her own hands killed his favourite war-horse, that he might be suitably provided to appear before Odin in the halls of Valhalla. She told Osric this, and Thordstein confirmed it, his dim eyes glistening with pride at his true Danish wife, as he said, "He hath blessed

her ever since, for thus winning him entrance to
the halls of the heroes, and shall I disgrace her by
dying in my bed? Nay, nay, I will—"

Osric knew what he was about to utter—that he
would take his own life, to save his honour and
gain a blessed immortality; but he interrupted him
by saying, "I am skilled in the curing of wounds,
even to the joining of broken bones."

Thordstein looked at the monk curiously. "I
have heard ye monks are so skilled, but are ye a
true man? Thou hast no cause to show me kindness, for many a monastery have I helped to burn,
while the rest drove off the cattle and carried away
the corn," he said, frankly.

"I have vowed to obey the White Christ, who
hath commanded us to forgive our enemies, and
therefore do I ask thee now to let me bind up thy
wounds, and it may be thou wilt again be able to
bear armour."

"And burn a few more monasteries," said Thordstein, mischievously.

"Nay, I trust if thou art cured thou wilt thank
Him who cureth thee, for it is God alone who can
do this."

"If thy God can heal him of such wounds as
he hath, he must be greater than our gods," said
Thorgiva his wife, as she lifted the piece of wadmal, or coarse cloth, with which he was covered.
She looked at the monk eagerly, as he examined
the jagged cuts and bruises; but there was a far

WADMAL: *a heavy cloth woven of yarn*

worse injury than any of these, for one arm lay helpless at his side, and Thorgiva knew that the bone was broken. Osric soon discovered this too, but by this time the limb was so much swollen that he saw it would be useless to try to set it yet.

"I would thou hadst sent for me last night," he said, and then he sent Thorgiva for a horn of cold water.

Before applying any remedies, however, he told his patient that it was absolutely necessary for his cure that he should ask the help and blessing of God upon what he was about to apply, and that it would also be necessary for him to abstain from all further participation in the festival now being held in honour of Thor. Thordstein demurred to these conditions at first, but Thorgiva persuaded him to yield to the monk's prescription, and so Osric kneeled down by the bedside and pleaded with God that He would heal and save, not only the body, but the soul of this man, who lay wounded almost unto death.

He then proceeded to dress Thordstein's wounds and apply remedies for reducing the swelling and inflammation of the broken limb; and with a promise to come again in the evening and see how he progressed, he returned to the brethren in the wood, that they might set about looking for a spot where they could at once commence their work of building, or timbering, as it was called in those days, when the building was to be entirely

DEMURRED: *objected*

of wood. Before night they had selected a suitable spot near the center of Ea, on a slightly rising ground, sufficiently near to both wood and water for them to be of easy access, and yet far enough away from the sacred grove and altar of Thor that the pagan festivals should not interrupt their daily service in the church, or they be brought into too close neighbourhood with these heathen worshipers to provoke them to any act of violence. And yet they were near enough to see the smoke continually rising from the ever-burning fire that was kept there, and which would serve to remind them of the purpose for which their abbey had been built—to quench this sacred flame of Thor's and teach this war-god's war-loving worshipers to become the followers of the Prince of Peace.

Having chosen a site for the abbey, their next care was to enclose some of the meadowland at once, that they might sow a few roots and vegetables for winter use. It was too late to sow any kind of grain, and so they must trust in God for bread; but if they had a plentiful supply of vegetables, they might with these perhaps purchase some oatmeal and flour for porridge.

Of the mechanical art of building Osric knew nothing, but one of his companions did, and so he took the direction of affairs now, drew the plan, measured out the ground, marked which trees should be cut down by the workmen; for the thane readily lent the services of his slaves, and they joyfully set to work to help the monks, for they were for the most part Angles and Christians, and could give the monks much valuable information concerning the state of the country previous to the coming of the Danes.

They had been forced to follow the religion of their masters lately, the Danes saying their god Thor must be the best, since he was the strongest, and had enabled them to conquer the Angles; and this unanswerable argument had been made the means of compelling them to give up their Christian worship, many of them being sacrificed as offerings to the idol if they attempted any resistance.

They heard too that many of the younger warriors among the Danes had taken Saxons or Angles for their wives, since there were none of their own countrywomen to be had here, and these still held secretly their belief in the Christian faith, although they joined with their husbands in the pagan festivals. Doubtless by and by, when the church was timbered, these would find courage to come and listen to the sermons and join in the services, and they might bring their children and induce their husbands to come with them.

This brought to Osric's mind another portion of their monastic work as doubtless necessary, although he somewhat despised it, and that was to build a school, where these children could be taught to recite the Lord's Prayer and the Apostles' Creed, and also some of the Scripture poetry of

MONASTIC: *relating to a monastery or monks*
APOSTLES' CREED: *an early formal statement of Christian beliefs*

Cædmon. A few might go further than this, and learn to read and write in Danish or Saxon; but Osric esteemed these arts very lightly. The Creed and the Lord's Prayer contained the whole of Osric's theology; and if children and, for that matter, older people too, knew these perfectly and believed them thoroughly, they needed nothing more in the way of learning. Nay, learning, except in the case of those like his beloved Egbert, who were clearly not strong enough for manual labour, often engrossed the time and energies of those who would be much better employed in cultivating the land or in building and repairing the abbeys.

This was Osric's view of the matter; but he knew that others thought differently, and he was willing to believe that God at least tolerated this learning, that took men beyond even the Scriptures and the poetical translation of them, which was the most common and popular form of teaching their truths; and therefore, if God was thus merciful and tolerant of such strange vagaries as a preference for books above agriculture, why, he would be the same, however much he might despise them in his secret heart.

So a school was to be added to the abbey; and then, looking round on all the hopeful signs of their mission being a success, beyond even their most sanguine expectations, he began to look forward to the time when Egbert should join them.

VAGARIES: *whims*
SANGUINE: *confident*

Chapter VII

The Wounded Warrior

THAT Thordstein would never recover from his wounds was accepted as a foregone conclusion by his friends and countrymen, who had witnessed the duel and knew how much he was hurt, and greatly pitied him that he was compelled to yield at last with a remnant of life still left in him.

"Thorgiva will help him to attain the hall of Odin," said one of the neighbours, as Osric was leaving the house one day.

The monk looked as though he did not understand, and the man hastened to explain what he meant. "There is in Sweden a rock so high that no animal can fall from the top and live. Here men betake themselves when they are unhappy. From this place all our ancestors who die not in battle have departed to Odin, therefore it is called the hall of Odin. Now Thordstein could not reach the top of such a hill, even if it were here, without the help of some friend, and it would be a sacred duty for someone to carry him thither; but

now, since we are in the Angles' land, and not our
own Sweden, Thordstein must go by another path
to Odin, and Thorgiva will lead him, like a true
Danish woman."

Osric could scarcely repress a shudder as he listened, for he knew all too well what the man meant,
and knew also that Thorgiva, so kind and attentive
to her husband, so careful to follow all his direc-
tions, would be capable of doing this thing which
the man hinted at, and which it was evident her
neighbours expected she would do. Had she not
driven her former husband back to certain death,
and gloried in the deed? and might he not come
perhaps the next day and find his patient had been
helped to the hall of Odin by his wife? For unfortunately Thordstein was not recovering as his physician could wish, and both he and Thorgiva knew
that there was little or no favourable progress.

Could it be that, in his prayers at the sick man's
bedside, he was thinking more than he ought
of the remedies he was about to apply, and
therefore trusted too little to the power of God
which could alone make them efficacious? He
himself believed that if these prayers were omitted
the remedies would do harm rather than good,
and this he firmly impressed upon the mind
of his patient, who otherwise would hardly have
submitted to the ordeal each day. As it was, he
looked upon it sometimes as almost an act of
treachery to submit to be cured by the God of

EFFICACIOUS: *effective*

the Christians, and he said as much to his wife one day. But Thorgiva shook her head thoughtfully. "I have listened to the monk's prayers," she said, "and I would fain know more of this God. If it be that He cures thee of such wounds as thou hast, I shall begin to think He is not to be despised, for it was He who helped the Saxons and their King Alfred at Ethandune, where hundreds of our warriors fell who were devoted worshipers of Thor."

"Then dost thou think that the White Christ is as great as our war-god, as strong as our Thunderer?" asked her husband in surprise.

"Nay, I know not yet, my Thordstein; let us wait awhile, and we may see;" and she turned her head aside as she spoke, to avoid her husband's look of startled astonishment. That Thordstein should linger so long soon became the talk of the neighbourhood; none the less because the stranger monk continued to go each day, and sometimes twice a day, to dress his wounds, and see whether there was any sign of improvement, and also that his wife did not seem to grow weary of nursing him, and spoke little of what passed when the monk was there.

The priest of Thor had treated the monks with the greatest contempt, but finding now that they were attracting some notice, he warned his followers against being too near these strangers, as they would practice magical arts against them if they placed themselves within their power. The people were greatly alarmed when they heard this, for many of them had gone to the mead-hall to hear Osric tell the wonderful story of his God coming down from heaven and dwelling among men—a story more wonderful than their own sagas told of the coming of Odin to the North.

Of course they told Thorgiva of the priest's warning, and advised her not to let the monk come into her dwelling again, as the arts of magic were always more powerful in a close building than in the open air.

But, to their surprise, Thorgiva only smiled as she said, "This monk is a true man, I trow, or he would have used this magic upon us at the mead-hall, when we laughed and mocked at his God for being merciful and tender."

"Well, thou dost not believe in any god being so weak and pitiful as—nay, nay, Thorgiva, I know thee well enough for a true Danish woman who dost despise pity. Pity? mercy? who ever heard of such words from a Dane? who ever heard of mercy and pity from Odin, the father of slaughter, and Thor, our god of war? What did we tell our heroes, who are now in the halls of Odin, when they fled before the face of the Saxons? Did we not drive them back, in the name of our gods, to take their wounds in front, and die like warriors?" and the fierce eyes blazed, and she raised her right arm, as though she herself would wield sword and battle-axe in emulation of the men.

But Thorgiva only smiled rather sadly at the recollection her friend's words brought to her mind,
as she said, "Perhaps thou dost think I am growing weak, unworthy to be called a Dane, because
I do not—"

"Nay, nay, thou art a true Viking's daughter, and
will help Thordstein to the hall of Odin by and
by, if he does not soon get well," interrupted her
companion; and then she held a whispered con-
versation with Thorgiva, promising to come and
see her again in the course of the day, and keep
her company, as she must be very dull just now.

The next time Osric lifted the wooden latch that
secured the door of Thordstein's house, a strange
woman came forward, and at the same moment a
feeble wail was heard from a recess in one corner
of the room, and as he approached the bed where
Thordstein lay, the man seemed suddenly to have
forgotten his pain, and instead of the grumbling,
impatient exclamation with which he usually
greeted the monk, he said, "Our baby came in the
night. Thorgiva hath got a son to nurse now, so
that I must soon get well, or—or depart to the halls
of Odin," he said, more slowly.

"Nay, nay, but I trust that God will bless the remedies I am using, and that thou wilt get well again,
and live to see thy son grow to be a man—and—"

"And a hero," interrupted Thordstein. "Every
Dane must be a hero, or he is not worthy to be a
Dane."

"Well, let us hope the babe will be a hero," said the monk pleasantly, as he proceeded to get the bandages ready; but he sighed as he spoke, for what hope was there for Saxon England with these hero warriors in the midst of her? It seemed to Osric that the growing cares and discouragements of this mission were already beyond his strength; for the countenance that the thane had at first given him had been withdrawn through the influence of the priest of Thor, and he was now forbidden to go to the mead-hall to preach, for fear he should exercise magical arts upon the people. He had hoped great things would result too from his being able to cure Thordstein quickly; but somehow he did not get on as he had hoped and expected, although there was certainly some slight improvement, and if the man would only be patient he might be perfectly cured by and by. And then, as he thought of this, he sighed more deeply than ever, for what use would Thordstein make of his restored health, but to pillage and burn and destroy the homes and churches and monasteries of flourishing Mercia? There were other causes too for discomfort. Elswitha, the fugitive in the forest, was still unable to walk and escape wholly out of the power of her foes, and if she were discovered now, it would be known who had befriended her, and might destroy all their hopes of establishing themselves in Ea.

COUNTENANCE: *encouragement, support*

It was not often that Osric gave way to depression of any kind, but as he walked through the silent glades of the forest, and thought of Thordstein and Thorgiva, and how little response he had won from them to anything he had taught, and how the thane had suddenly seemed to avoid him, he could not help feeling discouraged.

He was going to see Elswitha now, or rather her foot, for he had not been for a day or two, and one of the brethren had told him it was worse, and the girl was quite unable to move. Of course she would tease him with complaints about the pain she suffered, and her fears lest she should be re-taken, and just now Osric felt that his own burden of care was almost more than he could carry, and so before he reached the sheltered nook where the girl lay hidden, he fell upon his knees and prayed for strength to bear the burdens that were laid upon him.

While he was thus kneeling he heard the sound of singing, and his heart almost stood still with affright. He had invaded the home of the forest-spirits, and they were mocking at his prayer, and he, who had never quailed before mortal man, felt almost afraid to look round, lest he should fall into their hands and be carried off bodily, nobody knew where.

But as he kneeled thus in breathless terror, he gradually came to understand that if it was a spirit singing, they were words that a mortal man could

TEASE: *irritate*

understand, and moreover that the words were those of their holy poet Cædmon, who had versified the greater portion of the Bible, thus rendering it easy to be learned by those who could never hope to possess such a costly treasure as a copy of the Scriptures, and could not read it even if they had obtained it. Softly, and yet with a ringing note of triumph in the tone, came the words to Osric:—

> "Now should we all heaven's guardian King exalt,
> The power and counsels of our Maker's will,
> Father of glorious works, Eternal Lord.
> He from old 'stablished the origin
> Of every varied wonder. First He shaped,
> For us the sons of earth, heaven's canopy,
> Holy Creator. Next this middle realm,
> This earth; the bounteous guardian of mankind,
> The everlasting Lord, for mortals formed.
> Ruler omnipotent."

This simple Anglo-Saxon poetry, the harmony of which depended chiefly upon the alliteration, or the recurrence of the initial letters of the words—surely this would not be sung by forest-spirits, and Osric breathed more freely, and ventured to rise from his knees and look round him. But although he had made up his mind that the singer was of mortal birth, he started with surprise when he saw Elswitha leaning against a tree only a few yards off; for they were some little distance from her hiding-place. She started too when she saw the monk, for she feared he would be angry

VERSIFIED: *put to verse*

to find her there, and singing too, and she said in a tone of apology, "I could not help it," and then she lifted her soft blue eyes to heaven and smiled so sweetly, that Osric began to be in doubt as to whether Elswitha were not an angel, or one of the forest-spirits after all, who had just assumed a mortal shape to tempt and destroy him the more surely. So, before venturing any nearer, or even to speak to the beautiful singer, he crossed himself and repeated a prayer that he had been told was all-potent in making evil spirits fly, and he almost expected to see this girl vanish as he repeated the talismanic words.

But no! Elswitha stood quite still, her eyes meekly cast down now, and her injured foot raised a little way from the ground, as she leaned against the tree for support. So the big brave man took courage to look at her again, and said slowly, "My daughter, how camest thou hither? the brethren told me thy foot was no better yesternight."

The girl looked at her foot and smiled. "I had almost forgotten I had a foot," she said; "my heart was so full of joy and gladness, that I scarce knew I was walking, until I came here."

"And wherefore art thou so glad?" asked Osric, in some astonishment. The girl had always been very silent when he had visited her—silent, but patient and humble, listening reverently to all he said, but rarely speaking herself; so that to see her thus walking and singing, when he expected to

TALISMANIC: *magically protecting*

see her lying still and groaning with pain, seemed little short of a miracle, and he made up his mind that for her a miracle had been wrought, and that she was one specially favoured of Heaven, when she said simply, in answer to his question, "How can I help feeling glad, with such a glorious Father in heaven?" and the girl lifted her eyes and looked upwards at the blue sky as it shone down between the glancing leaves of the trees.

"But how dost thou know He is thy Father, my daughter?" said Osric.

"Is He not the Father of all these glorious works—this sky, and sun, and lovely clouds, and of this earth, and trees, and all we see; and are we not His sons? Did not the White Christ die to redeem us? The holy noble bard Cædmon and—and—forgive me, holy father, if I am bold, but I know—I know He loves me. Yes, the White Christ loves poor Elswitha, and would not let them send me to the halls of Odin, but hath saved me for Himself, all for Himself. Dost thou wonder now that I am glad?" she asked.

But Osric could only shake his head in silent amazement. Elswitha was not a poor slave girl after all, then, it seemed, but a saint—a special favourite of Heaven; and Osric now felt inclined to kneel before her, for already it seemed that he had caught something of her spirit, and his burden of care was lifted.

"I could not help singing," she went on, seeing the monk was silent, and lifting her rapt face to

GLANCING: *reflecting light*

his. Dost thou not hear the birds singing the same song, praising our Father for His goodness, and Christ for His love?"

Of course Osric took her words literally, and quite believed that she could hear more than he or any mortal could in these birds' songs; and he was ready to believe too that now there was no danger of her being discovered by her enemies, for if one happened to be passing as near as he was when she was singing, he would be smitten with sudden deafness, so that he might not hear, or with blindness, so that he should not see her.

But these thoughts suggested to his mind another question. "Art thou not afraid when the sun sets and the stars come out?" he said.

"Why should I be afraid then? If I wake in the night, I look up into their brightness, and I think they are just little bits of the bright heaven where God is, that He has put there that we may never forget Him, and how He loves us; and then just over there it seems as though the wonderful ladder that Cædmon tells about was let down again, and I can see the angels coming down and going up as Jacob did. Oh no, I am not afraid of the stars, God's stars, when I have escaped from Odin."

How strange all this sounded to Osric, how far removed from earth this girl seemed to be in his imagination, we can hardly comprehend, because we know nothing of the hard and fast lines, the set and rigid rules, within which the religious thought

of that day was confined. Men fasted and prayed
and praised by rule on set days of the week and
at certain hours of the day, and fashioned their
thought of God in somewhat the same manner in
these infant days of the Church; and so for one to
spring upwards in spontaneity of soul and throw
off these swaddling-clothes, as every now and then
one and another did do, was looked upon as something little short of a miracle, and the recipients of
such grace and favour were at once exalted to the
dignity of saints in the eyes of their friends.

So the longer Elswitha talked, the more convinced Osric became that she was one of these favoured ones, sent specially by God to bless their
mission, and that it was their duty no longer to
think of sending her away, but to build her here a
little hermitage, which by and by might grow and
flourish as an establishment of nuns, over whom
she would preside as the gentle abbess.

Chapter VIII

The Parley

THE building of the hermitage occupied so much of Osric's time and attention now, that although he went in to dress Thordstein's wounds each day, he did not linger there longer than was actually necessary, and he failed to see that the people whom he met in his walks either avoided him altogether or looked at him questioningly, suspiciously.

In listening to the story of Elswitha's life, and witnessing her calm faith and loving trust in God, he had been lifted so far above the depression that had threatened almost to crush him only a short time before, that he saw nothing of all this. Their mission to Ea would be, must be, a success, and these fierce Danes would soon turn from their love of war and learn the arts of peace.

If his mind had not been so preoccupied with these sanguine hopes and anticipations, he could not have failed to see the malignant scowl cast upon him by the white-robed priest of Thor, as he passed the sacred grove one day on his way to Thordstein's cottage.

There had been some improvement in his patient at last, and Thorgiva, who had begun to get about again, and nurse her husband, as well as her baby, was looking forward to the time when he would be able to take their first-born in his arms, and go with her to see the abbey and the church that were being timbered.

She was telling Osric of this, when a neighbour suddenly opened the door, and whispered something in her ear. Thorgiva turned pale, and coming to the monk she said, "Wilt thou baptize me, holy father?"

Her husband looked astonished, and the monk not less so.

"Baptize thee," repeated Thordstein; "why wilt thou forsake the worship of Thor?"

"Because—because I believe in the God of the Christians," she said slowly; and then turning to Osric she said, "Holy father, wilt thou baptize me now?"

"Now? here?" exclaimed the monk.

"Yes, yes, at once, this minute," said Thorgiva.

"Nay, but that cannot be; I must know of thy mind and belief in this matter," said Osric, wondering what could have happened, to make the woman wish for this so suddenly.

"Then if I wait awhile, wait until the new church is built, and the worship of the White Christ begins there, thou wilt baptize me then?" said Thorgiva, placing her hands upon the monk's arm.

"Then that is why thou wouldst not name our child after our Danish fashion," said her husband.

"I could not have the child named for Thor or Odin, when I meant he should be God's man," said Thorgiva.

Osric looked at the unconscious face of the little child, and then at his strange mother. Could it be she was really in earnest?—she, the fierce cruel woman who had driven her husband to certain death! Could she be really in earnest? He could not long indulge in these thoughts, for while still filled with wonder he suddenly heard a noisy crowd in the distance, and the next minute Thorgiva, clasping her baby in her arms, exclaimed, "We are lost, we are lost, we must go to Odin. Would that I had been baptized, that I might go to the kingdom thou hast told of, where the God of love and mercy doth reign! Fly, holy father, or they will kill thee, as well as us!"

Thordstein raised himself in bed, and gazed wildly around. "Who will kill thee, my Thorgiva—thee and our precious babe? Give me the child, and—"

"Give me the battle-axe, and help me hold the door!" said Osric; for he could distinguish by the shouts of the crowd upon what errand they were bent, and it was useless for him to think of escape now. He would defend this helpless household, and sell his life dearly, at any rate. And the next minute he had girded on Thordstein's shield, and stood ready with his battle-axe in the little narrow doorway, waiting for the approach of the crowd.

They were evidently taken aback at seeing the monk thus armed and ready to meet them, and one or two who had been most eager to press forward now fell behind, and the priest of Thor was left in the forefront of the crowd. He, in virtue of his sacred office, did not bear arms, and Osric would not think of striking an unarmed foe, so he lowered his battle-axe, and stood waiting for the priest to speak, while *he* thought some of the warriors ought to rush forward and commence the fight.

At length, finding the crowd was waiting, Osric said, loud enough for all to hear, "Our God hath a controversy with thy Thor; or rather with you his worshipers is it!"

"We care nought for the pitiful God of the Saxons, but we have come to rescue Thordstein and Thorgiva from thy magical arts," said the priest, without waiting to hear all the monk had to say.

"Of the arts of magic I know nothing," said Osric; "I have nought to do with sorceress or prophetess, and could not use their arts, even if I would. But wherefore shouldst thou think I had used magic with Thordstein and Thorgiva?" he asked.

"Is not Thordstein a hero and a warrior, and should he not be drinking strong ale and eating boar's flesh in the halls of Odin, instead of lying there dying by inches, to go to the accursed Hela in Niflheim, whose table is hunger and her knife starvation, where there is neither meat nor drink, as in the halls of Valhalla?"

"And wherefore should he be in the halls of Odin, and not among the warriors here in East Anglia?" asked Osric, who was quite willing to use his tongue instead of his battle-axe, and hoped they might settle the dispute by argument instead of fighting.

"Among the warriors!" repeated the priest of Thor. "Never since thy coming among us hath Thordstein been among our warriors."

"Nay, but he hath been wounded in single combat, as thou knowest; hath received his wounds honourably, although they are healing but slowly."

"Healing! Thou knowest his wounds are not healing, monk; and yet thou hast by thy magical arts changed the nature of his noble wife Thorgiva, that she will not help her husband, hath refused to give him a place in the halls of the heroes."

"But Thordstein is recovering; he is much better," said Osric, calmly.

But the heathen priest only shook his head, and screamed the more loudly in his mad passion, "Thou art changing the nature of a hero and a Viking, or he would not lie there a nithing, and—"

But at that word Osric had raised his battle-axe threateningly, for not even from a priest would

NIFLHEIM: *Viking "hell"—a place for those who did not die in battle, ruled by Hela, queen of the underworld*
NITHING: *same as nidling; a coward*

he take that execrable word of reproach. Several others too in the crowd raised their voices against that.

"Thordstein is no nithing!" shouted one.

"Thordstein is a hero and a warrior!" said another.

"He is a Dane and Viking, worthy of the halls of Valhalla, and no nithing!" cried a third; and amid the shouts and uproar, nothing that Osric said could be heard for some few minutes.

At length they understood that although Thordstein had not heard the insulting epithet, Osric was willing to wield his battle-axe, if a champion could be found for the priest of Thor; for of course he could not fight himself: and thus the two champions might avenge the gratuitous insult. But, for a wonder, no one was found willing to be the champion of the priest. One or two volunteered to take up the quarrel for Thordstein, but the priest had gone a little too far in calling one whose well-known bravery had won him such a wife as Thorgiva a 'nithing;' and his influence over the crowd was gone.

Pushing him aside with scant ceremony now, one or two of the warriors pressed to the front, and said to Osric, "Canst thou tell us, monk, why Thorgiva hath forgotten her duty as a Danish woman and the wife of a warrior, that she should let Thordstein lie like this, to go to Hela in Niflheim at last?"

Thorgiva had laid her baby on the bed beside

EXECRABLE: *detestable*
EPITHET: *name or title*
GRATUITOUS: *unnecessary*

her husband, and came to the door in time to hear this question. The monk would have kept her out of the sight of that excited mob just now, but she would not be kept back. Drawing herself up to her full height, she pushed her way to Osric's side.

"Who hath dared to say that I am not a true Danish wife?" she demanded, looking round fearlessly upon the crowd.

"We asked why thou hast not done thy duty to Thordstein, as thou didst to him who is now in the halls of Valhalla."

For a moment Thorgiva grew pale, and her voice trembled slightly as she said, "Because, because I love my husband, and am a Christian—a believer in the God of mercy and love; therefore I have not been to the festival of Thor, and will not slay Thordstein."

As brave as any warrior in the crowd did she stand and make this declaration, that almost took their breath away as they heard it. Thorgiva a Christian! Thorgiva, the sternest, bravest woman in the Ea, who roused her companions in the camp and drove back their panic-stricken husbands to face the foe again and die like heroes, with all their wounds in front! Thorgiva a worshiper of the despised God of the Saxons, the God of love and mercy! Surely they could not have heard aright. Their ears must have played them false for once. It seemed altogether so incredible, that they could only look at each other in mute, blank astonishment for a few minutes.

At length one of them found his tongue. "Hast thou been baptized, like our king, who now calls himself Æthelstan?" he asked.

"Nay, I have but now made known to the monk that I believe in his God," she replied; "but thou knowest that I have not named my son for Thor's man, and it is because I would have him give hands to the White Christ, and be His man, for this will I try to make him, if he live."

"Then thou dost mean to be baptized, Thorgiva?" said one of her old friends.

"I have already vowed in my heart to renounce Thor and live to the White Christ. Wherefore then should I not be baptized?" she asked. They could not tell, but as yet they could not get over the astonishment her bold avowal had caused. True, their king had been baptized, and thirty of his chief officers with him, and he had promised for them that they too should become Christians; but such promises and such Christianity as this was altogether different from what Thorgiva's avowal intended. Guthrum, or Æthelstan, had been glad to make any terms with the victorious King of Wessex, the Saxon Alfred, for he and his Danes were entirely at Alfred's mercy—had been on the verge of starvation, without hope of supplies reaching them, and he was glad to promise anything at the moment, and East Anglia was a prize worth being baptized for, to say nothing of life and liberty.

But Thorgiva had no such temptation to forsake the religion of her ancestors. What if Thor was no god at all, as some few of the boldest among them had lately been heard to whisper? They were no worse than their ancestors, who worshiped the war-god and served him truly with lance and battle-axe and never questioned his power. Perhaps he was not as powerful as they had once imagined; but then, if he was not, there were the festivals held in his honour, when there was feasting and merry-making, and friends met together who would never otherwise see each other.

This was some of the reasoning, some of the self-communing, that went on in the minds of the crowd as they pondered over Thorgiva's strange determination to be a Christian. It was clearly incomprehensible, except upon one theory—that she had been bewitched, and this was the conclusion arrived at by most of them.

But one or two, indignant at the insult that had been offered to Thordstein in calling him "nithing," had turned away, which caused a division in the general feeling; and at last the crowd broke up, without a blow having been struck.

With a sigh of relief Osric laid down the battle-axe, thankful that he could do so without having used it, and Thorgiva, taking her baby from the bed, where she had hidden it, covered its unconscious face with her warm kisses.

"We have escaped this time, baby," she said.

"Yes, for a little while," said Thordstein; "but it will not be for long, if thou dost not go to the feast of Thor next week."

"I will never join in the worship of Thor again," said his wife calmly, but firmly.

"But wherefore, Thorgiva, dost thou—"

"Have I not told thee I do not believe in Thor?" interrupted Thorgiva, as her husband paused.

"But—but many do not believe in him now, as they once did, who still take a sacrifice now and then, and go to his feast, Thorgiva."

"What dost *thou* say, monk?—can I go to the feast of Thor and yet serve the White Christ in the abbey church?" she asked.

But Osric shook his head. "Nay, thou must choose whom thou wilt serve, Thor or the White Christ, for thou canst not serve both."

Thordstein looked a little offended at this speech. "Thy White Christ should be glad of the worship of a Danish woman like Thorgiva, and suffer her to come as it best pleaseth *her*," he said.

"Our great and gracious God doth welcome all who will come to Him; but they must come and worship Him wholly. He will not accept a divided heart. Nay, how canst thou worship thy cruel god of war and love our Prince of Peace, the Lord Jesus Christ?"

"And, Thordstein, I am tired of war; I want to

learn about this Prince of Peace. I want our boy to be a man of peace."

Had she said she desired her babe to be blind, or a cripple, it would scarcely have astonished her husband more.

"A man of peace!" he repeated, "a man of peace, and he is a Dane! What art thou saying, Thorgiva? What hath a man to live for, but the glory of the battlefield? Why do I lie here day after day, instead of departing mine own way to the hall of Odin, but that I hope to leave a well-covered shield to our boy, and the name of a hero who delighted in slaughter like Odin himself? Ah, monk, I hope to see many a house and church and monastery burning in thy Saxon England yet. It is this hope that cheers me as I lie here," he added.

Osric sighed, and Thorgiva looked perplexed; but neither of them spoke for a minute or two, until Thorgiva said, "But thou wilt let me bring up our babe as the man of the Prince of Peace?"

"Thou mayest follow thy will in this, Thorgiva; but I tell thee, if thou trainest him for the White Christ, I will teach him, as all our boys are taught, that there is nothing in the world like the glory of war. I have nought to say against the White Christ," he went on; "I would worship Him in the church myself, but that all my ancestors have served Thor, and we Danes know not the meaning of this word Peace. Monk, if thou hadst come to us with any other message; if thou hadst told us that thy God delighted in war, as Thor doth, we should have listened, I trow; for I will tell thee this, that if it were not for the feast that followed there would be few worshipers at the festivals of our gods. They do not satisfy us, as they did our fathers; our souls crave for more than the priest can give us, and it may be we should find something for this hunger in our nature in this Christianity which ye teach, if thy God were a God of war instead of peace."

"But, Thordstein, if the Lord Christ were full of anger and malice and revenge and cruelty, were a God of slaughter, like Thor, dost thou think He would have healed thee of thy deadly wounds, as He now is doing? Would He have sent me with a message, think you, or fiery thunderbolts to destroy ye Danes from off the face of the earth, for the evil which thou hast done here in our Saxon England?"

"I know not why thy God should not do as thou sayest if He is able, for we are Vikings, land-ravagers, and we have laid waste this land of thine."

"I will tell thee, Thordstein, why He hath not pursued thee with thunder and lightnings, that should kill thee all like insects: it is because He is a God of mercy and love, and He would fain have ye Danes believe it, and turn from the false gods whom thy fathers have served, and worship Him, the only God."

Osric bade Thordstein ponder over these words, and then rose to take his departure.

Chapter IX

Whispering Spirits

OSRIC went home, feeling both anxious and hopeful—anxious because of what had occurred, but very hopeful that these Danes would receive the Gospel before long, since they were growing dissatisfied with the old idol-worship. As he drew near to the little stream that meandered in and out in a serpentine course here and there about the Ea, he saw brother Redwald coming hurriedly towards him in great excitement and with an eager, flushed countenance. Osric wondered what could have happened, but before he could utter a word or seek any explanation, Redwald exclaimed, "My brother, God hath put the fear of us even into the spirits of the waters and the forest, so that they cannot harm us."

But Osric held up his finger and uttered a warning, "Hush!" for they were close to the stream and not very far from the wood, and these unknown but dreaded beings might resent being spoken of in this way, if they overheard it, and Redwald had

SERPENTINE: *snake-like*

forgotten the usual caution used, and spoke aloud instead of in a whisper.

He smiled, however, at Osric's start of affright, and said, "There is nought to be feared, for they cannot harm us; I have overheard two of them talking today, and though they have tried to break my line and nets, they could not do it, nor can they hinder the fish from coming to me."

"Thou didst hear them say that?" uttered Osric in an awestruck whisper, looking at the young priest in amazement.

"Come, let us walk on, and I will tell thee about this. As thou knowest, it is the day for sending our tribute of fish to the thane, and so I came forth to do this, and had sat for some time in a little sheltered hollow where I could hear nothing but the murmur of the little river and the whisper of the leaves on the trees. But at length I heard a sound like, and yet unlike, these whisperings and murmurings, and at last a voice said, 'He is invading our kingdom; he will rob us of our power.' 'He hath robbed us of it,' replied another voice, in a soft plaintive tone. 'I have tried to break his net, but I cannot, or to entangle his line so that he should get nothing from my kingdom in the water, but it is all a failure;' and then there was a sobbing sound, as though the water-spirits were shedding tears."

"It is wonderful," said Osric; "God hath been very gracious to thee, my brother, to open thine

PLAINTIVE: *sorrowful*

ears to such things as these, for mere mortal sens-
es can never detect when these spirits are near."

"When the water-spirit had finished her complaint, the forest-spirit said, 'My rights too have
been invaded by these servants of the great God,
and I have tried to throw down the trees they were
chopping, so that they might kill them, but I too
have failed. What are we to do now?'"

"And didst thou hear the answer?" asked Osric
anxiously, for he never doubted that this conversa-
tion had really taken place, and the priest been
specially endowed to hear it. But Redwald had
failed to hear anymore; something had occurred
to distract his attention from the sounds of the
breeze among the leaves and the rippling of the
waters, and his imagination could not conjure up
any more voices. That he believed he had heard
actual voices was beyond a doubt; he was too sin-
cere and too devout to pretend to anything of the
kind, and the brethren knew it, so that no one
among them thought of doubting this marvelous
story.

But in the midst of their rejoicing over this power to defeat the machinations of their supernatural foes, they learned that mortal enemies were
still active, and now threatened greater opposition
than ever.

While they were eating their frugal midday
meal in the shed that at present served for a refectory, they were startled by the sound of a woman's

MACHINATIONS: *plotting*
REFECTORY: *dining hall*

voice just outside, and on going to the entrance they saw Thorgiva with the child in her arms.

She held it at once towards Osric, and with panting breath uttered, "Take him and baptize him for the White Christ; they want to make him Odin's man, but I have saved him!" and then, without waiting for the monk's answer, she turned and sped homeward again.

Osric told the brethren how anxious she had been about the child before, and they suspected now that some of her friends and relatives, knowing of her determination, were resolved to prevent the little one receiving Christian baptism by forcibly performing the pagan rite customary at naming a child.

Entering heartily into the anxious mother's feeling, Osric carried the baby into the unfinished church, and some water being brought, the little one was baptized, in the name of the Father, and of the Son, and of the Holy Ghost—the firstfruits of their mission to East Anglia.

The child was named Æthelstan, after the king, for in her hurry Thorgiva had forgotten to say what she wished his name to be, and so Osric chose this one.

The little Æthelstan did not approve of the change of nurses, and cried lustily for his mother soon after she had left him; but this did not trouble the brethren at first, although they felt very awkward in handling their new charge, and held him as though there was imminent peril of his falling to pieces if they were not extremely careful. But all their care did not stay or even lessen the child's screams, and before the ceremony was over his shrieks had grown so piercing and loud that the poor monks were in momentary fear of a rabble rout from the village coming to drag him out of their hands.

But the minutes that seemed almost like hours slowly passed, and no one came, not even his mother; and when at last the baby had screamed until quite exhausted, and then fallen asleep, Osric ventured to lay him down on a wolf-skin, setting Redwald to watch by his side while he went in search of Thorgiva. He thought he should meet her on the road, and felt very vexed when he reached the village and still she did not come; for what were they to do with the child if he woke and screamed again? Full of these thoughts, he went on until he had reached her home, but no one answering his summons at the door, he opened it and went in. For a minute or two he could see nothing in the dim light that came from the single eye-hole in the wall, but he stumbled over something a few steps from the threshold, and stooping he picked up Thordstein's battle-axe, and the next minute his hand had touched that of his patient. Groping his way back to the door by which he had entered, he opened it, and then saw signs of a recent struggle, for Thordstein lay on the floor dead, while close

STAY: *stop*

to him lay Thorgiva, who had evidently tried to defend her husband, for she lay grasping a heavy mallet or club, and the floor and wall were bespattered with blood. At first he thought Thorgiva was dead as well as her husband, but as he stooped over her and took the deadly weapon from her hand, she uttered a feeble moan, and then he saw that she had only fainted from loss of blood, for there was a gaping wound in her arm from which it was still flowing. He bound this up as quickly as he could, and then went to the door again, hoping to see some of the neighbours. But the place seemed to be deserted, and at last he lifted her to the bed where her husband had lain and applied such restoratives as he had at hand.

At length she opened her eyes, and murmured, "My baby! Oh, my baby!"

"The child is safe," said Osric; and then, as her eyes closed again, he contrived to move the body of her husband, so that she should not see it at once.

But it seemed that she knew what had happened, for as soon as she had fully regained consciousness she said, "They would not let thee cure my Thordstein, lest all should know that the White Christ is greater than Thor. They have sent him to the halls of Odin: he died like a hero and a warrior," she went on, forgetful for a moment of her new faith.

"Now thou must do my bidding, and be very quiet, for thy baby's sake," said Osric, as she was about to speak again. He was anxious to have the particulars of the murder, but it would not do for Thorgiva to tell him just now. He was perplexed to know what he ought to do for the best: if only they had a convent now, and some kind sisters to nurse her, she could be removed thither without difficulty. But what could a community of monks do with a sick woman and helpless infant?

In his perplexity he resolved to appeal to the thane for help, for Thorgiva certainly could not be left alone in her present condition. As he wended his way up the hill to the mead-hall he could not help remarking the almost deserted appearance of the place, and he wished that, instead of the spirits being powerless to harm them, as brother Redwald had heard they were, these fierce Danes could be brought under something like Christian subjection and civilization.

As he returned he felt more troubled and perplexed than ever, for the thane had declined to interfere in what was evidently a family feud, and advised that Thorgiva should be left to the mercy of her relatives, who would doubtless bury her husband with all due honour, and take care of her and her child, if she was not obstinate.

"If she is not obstinate," repeated Osric, as he slowly retraced his steps; "that means, she must not renounce the worship of Thor, or receive Christian baptism. I wonder whether it was to defend her that Thordstein grasped his battle-axe once more. It will be a satisfaction to his friends that he died

WENDED: *made*

with it in his hand—died in mortal combat after all. But Thorgiva will grieve, I doubt not;" and then there arose a question in the monk's mind. As she had been so anxious to become a Christian, she would doubtless wish that Thordstein should receive Christian burial, and Osric would not know what to do about this, since he had never renounced paganism or professed to accept Christianity.

But this difficulty had been solved during his absence, for, guessing probably that Thorgiva would wish him to be buried with Christian rites, his friends had been in and carried off the body while the monk was away, and she was bitterly bemoaning this when Osric returned. The monk tried to comfort her by speaking of her baby, and then asked whether she wished to be left there and have her baby brought to her, or whether she would like to be removed to a little shelter, to which he could take her, where she would have the companionship of a Christian woman, who would teach her many things concerning the Christian faith, and how a woman could serve the White Christ.

"Yes, take me there, if she will have me—me and my baby; I cannot go without my baby," she added.

It seemed as though this baby had quite transformed the fierce woman. Could it be that God had taught her to know something of Himself, that His love was not to be despised, through the love she bore to her child? But Osric could not linger to think of this; for if Thorgiva was to be removed, he must go for help; and doubtless the brethren would be anxiously expecting his return, for what would they do with the baby, if it woke before he got back? When he reached home, he heard to his dismay that it had awoken and begun screaming before he had been away ten minutes, and Redwald, in despair, had carried it to Elswitha, who had scarcely had it in her arms a minute before the child was quiet and looking up into her face with a smile.

"Ah, my brother, if thou art gifted to hear the unknown voices of spirits, it takes a woman-saint, I trow, to calm a crying baby; and it hath . occurred to me today that we need these same women-saints, for there are things needed that the wisest man cannot do so well as the poor women-folk, and instead of building a hermitage for Elswitha, where she may dwell alone with God, we need a house for sisters, that may be a refuge and a home."

But Redwald shook his head. "My brother, it were a sin to disturb such a saint as Elswitha, to call her from the contemplation of God to the mean poor cares of this earthly time. I would not have taken this babe to her, but that we feared it would die from screaming so violently."

"And what said she, our saint Elswitha?" asked Osric, who had begun to fear now that his thought of connecting her with earthly concerns was little short of profanation.

PROFANATION: *a violation of something sacred*

"Well, I was not a little surprised at the way she took the child from my arms—nay, snatched it from me, and almost covered it with kisses, which, strange to say, the babe seemed to understand, although it had failed to comprehend what I said; for it had no sooner got into her arms than its crying was stayed, and it looked up into her face and smiled."

"And what said she? thou didst tell her the story of the little one?" asked Osric.

"I looked to see her bless the child in a saintly fashion; but, instead of that, she said, 'Baby is hungry, I trow; wilt thou fetch some food, that I may feed it?'"

"At which thou wert still more perplexed, Redwald?" said Osric, with a smile; and then he told him what had happened to Thordstein, and that his widow must be removed to the hermitage as well as her baby.

But Redwald looked aghast at the proposal. "Thou wouldst force one of these filthy pagans into that sacred dwelling, that she may betray Elswitha to her enemies! Think of it, my brother, and—"

"But what am I—what are we to do for Thorgiva, if she cannot go to the hermitage?" said Osric, in perplexity. He had quite as much reverential regard for the gentle pious Elswitha as Redwald and the rest of the brethren, and, cut off from the usual society of women, these monks needed to reverence the Virgin or some female saint as an outlet for the natural feeling of their hearts.

How far this feeling of reverence ought to be regarded in the matter of taking Thorgiva to be Elswitha's charge, Osric was at a loss to decide.

Of course she would have to descend to the homely humble duties of nursing the sick woman and her child, if they went there; and how far this would accord with her rapt contemplation of God and His glory and love and goodness Osric could not tell. Something, however, must be decided, and that very soon, for Thorgiva could not be left much longer alone in her desolated home, and so he resolved to go and see Elswitha, and tell her all that had happened, and hear what she would say about the matter.

So, telling Redwald to go and prepare a litter, in readiness to carry the wounded woman to some place of refuge, he turned aside into the path that would take him to the hermitage. He found Elswitha with the child asleep in her arms, and as he drew near the girl held up her finger warningly.

"But I must speak to thee, Elswitha," said Osric in a low tone, as he reached her side.

She looked up at him for a moment with a look of concern, but the next she was smiling upon the sleeping infant.

"Didst thou ever preach a sermon, holy father?" she asked.

"Preach a sermon!" repeated Osric. "I have preached many ere now; albeit I am not learned, and could only speak in homely fashion."

"Ah! but didst thou ever preach such a sermon as this baby king is preaching to us now?" she said, still gazing earnestly at the sweet unconscious face of the child.

"He is asleep," said Osric, wondering what she could mean.

"Yes! he hath fallen asleep, looking up with a smile in my face: I wonder whether we trust in our great Father as this little one trusteth in me."

"But—but we are grown men, and—"

"And God's babies, who know little more of our Father and His ways than this little one doth know of me or its mother."

"It is of his mother I came to speak to thee, Elswitha," said the monk, quickly. "Thou shalt tell me of this baby's sermon to thee afterwards, but now time is precious. Wilt thou be willing to nurse this child for awhile—this child and his mother?"

For a moment Elswitha turned pale as she said, "The woman is a Dane, I trow, and doubtless she would know me."

"But I do not think Thorgiva would betray thee,'" said Osric.

The girl started as she heard the name. "Thorgiva, the wife of Thordstein?" she said, in a questioning tone.

"Yes! Thordstein is dead, and Thorgiva is wounded."

For a moment Elswitha hesitated, but at length she said, "Fetch her hither, I will nurse her."

Chapter X

In the Wood

THORGIVA had been at her new home but a few hours, and had scarcely recovered from the fatigue of her removal, when a fresh anxiety seemed to take possession of her mind, and this was, whether her husband's relatives would accord him a funeral befitting his rank as a hero and warrior. She had scarcely seen Elswitha as yet, and quite forgot that as a Christian woman she could not be expected to have much sympathy with the rites and ceremonies of a pagan funeral; but so great was her anxiety lest Thordstein should not be properly mounted on his entrance to the halls of Odin, that she could not help calling Elswitha in the dusk of the evening to her bedside to talk about this.

"Art thou a Dane? Dost thou know aught of the manner of our burying the dead?"

"A little," answered Elswitha, trembling, as she looked down upon the tall gaunt woman, and wishing she could get away from her. But she dared not disobey that firm commanding voice, and those flashing fascinating eyes, that held her now, as they had held her before, spellbound.

"Thou knowest a little of our customs. Wilt thou go for me to the village, and bid them kill Thordstein's horse, and bury him in the barrow with his master? Tell them also to lay his own shield and battle-axe with him, for 'tis no white shield now that my Thordstein should carry to the halls of Odin. Remind them too of the flint, and all that he needeth for a light on his darksome journey. The monk bade me sleep, but I cannot sleep until I know all this is done, and that they will not bury my Thordstein on his face, like a slave. Go with all speed," she added, as Elswitha still seemed inclined to linger.

She could not but obey the command so far as to go outside; but once beyond the sight and hearing of Thorgiva, she threw herself upon the ground, and burst into an agony of sobs. "O Thou great God and Heavenly Father, help me to forgive, teach me to forgive my cruel enemy, who hath made my life desolate, and driven me to seek refuge in this forest! She and her cruel husband robbed me of father and mother, and would have sent my soul to Odin, but for these monks who rescued me; and now she bids me go to those who will never suffer me to escape from their hands again; and yet it would be better to go back to them and to slavery than do the evil deed that it is in my heart to perform. O God! Thou knowest the fierce angry passions that are in my heart; Thou knowest how I long to kill this woman, and send her to Odin with her husband, as her friends would doubtless have done, if the monks had not brought her here. Oh, why did she come? Why did they bring her to torture me, and raise all these evil thoughts in my heart?" And then sobs choked her utterance for awhile, and it seemed as though she was personally wrestling with the tempter who had whispered this evil suggestion to her.

There was one who overheard her prayer, and stood almost aghast as he listened. What had he done, what could he do, to rescue the poor girl from this temptation, and the misery Thorgiva's presence must cause her? He waited until she grew more calm, and then, making some noise to announce his approach, he stepped forward.

"I have brought some herb-tea for the woman," he said, "for it may be that her wounds will make her somewhat feverish. Is there aught I can do for thee, Elswitha? Tell me, shall I take this woman away from thee?"

For a moment the girl's lips quivered, as she said, "There is no convent here, no woman but myself, and so—so she shall stay, and I will nurse her. But I will ask thee to do an errand she hath bidden me to fulfill;" and then she told Osric of her anxiety concerning the funeral of her husband.

"Tell her thou didst meet me, and I bade thee say that Osric will do all that may be well for Thordstein's funeral. She doth believe in Odin still, I trow, since she hath such anxiety for her husband's being duly armed when he shall be laid in the grave."

"And is not Odin a—"

"Nay, nay, Elswitha, thou who art a Christian and almost a saint, dost thou not know that Odin is nought but a block of wood, or a lump of gold—a senseless, powerless idol, who can neither see nor hear, nor feel nor understand?"

"Thou dost think Odin is nought? I thought he was verily the god of the Danes, as the White Christ is of all Christians."

"Nay, nay; our God is King of all the earth, my sister; how can Odin then be the god of the Danes? and what think you we have come hither for, but to declare this truth to the Danes?"

"That God, even our God, will be the Saviour of these cruel Danes, who have desolated our homes, destroyed our churches, and dragged us to these pagan altars?" It was a truth hard to be believed by one who had suffered so cruelly at their hands, and Elswitha asked the question in doubting surprise. For a moment Osric wondered who could have taught Elswitha the Christian faith, and *not* taught her this. He forgot that she was little more than a child when first torn from her home; and that she should have held firmly the faith that there was in heaven a God for her, a God for Anglian and Saxon slaves as well as an Odin for Danes, was something more remarkable than that her ideas upon some things should grow confused from constantly hearing her haughty enemies vaunting the power of their god, the slaughter-loving Odin.

"It will not grieve thee, Elswitha, to hear that our Christ hath died to redeem Danes as well as Saxons and Angles," said Osric, after a pause.

"But the Danes will not have Him to be their Saviour; they despise a God of peace and love," she said.

"Thorgiva doth not. She doth desire now to serve the White Christ," said Osric.

"Thorgiva!" and Elswitha shuddered as she uttered the name.

"Did I not tell thee that she doth desire to be baptized, and wishes her little one to be no longer the child of Odin, the false god's sworn man, but the servant of our God and Saviour Jesus Christ?"

It was hard for the girl to believe that her fierce cruel enemy could ever be other than fierce and cruel, and she was ready to take up the fear now that she had come thither in search of her, until Osric assured her that this could not be; and then he related all that he knew about Thorgiva and her husband.

Elswitha felt somewhat relieved when she heard all these particulars; and a feeling of pity stole

VAUNTING: *boasting about*

into her heart as she thought of Thorgiva's grief for Thordstein's death, and her love for the little helpless babe which had lately come to her.

"I never thought Thorgiva could love even a little child," she said, looking up at the monk.

"It may be that God hath sent this baby to open her heart to Himself: from what she hath told me, she did once hate the very words "love" and "mercy," but since her little child hath come, and she hath learned their meaning, she no longer despiseth them."

"It may be as thou dost say, but it is strange, passing strange, that Thorgiva should be the first in Ea to declare herself a Christian."

"Thou wilt help her—wilt teach her, and do all—"

"Holy father, how can I do this, when she it was who sent my mother and father to Odin? They were hung up in the sacred grove, and their blood sprinkled upon the altar of Thor; and it was she, Thorgiva, who named them from among the captives as most fit for sacrifice."

"But, Elswitha, thy mother and father had served the Lord Christ, and dost thou think He would suffer any to snatch them from His all-powerful hands? Hast thou never heard the words, 'They shall never perish, neither shall any pluck them out of My hand?'[1] If Odin were a god, instead of a dumb idol, he could not rob the Lord Christ of His servants. Thy parents are with Him now, Elswitha. Thorgiva did but shorten their earthly

[1] JOHN 10:28

pain and travail, and give them a brighter inheritance in the land of light."

"Is it so—art thou sure of this, holy father?" gasped Elswitha, in the intensity of her feeling.

"My sister! thou hast heard of the Holy Scriptures—the Word of God Himself—as translated by the holy and venerable monk Bede into our Saxon tongue?"

Elswitha faintly answered, "Yes."

"Then I tell thee that these words are the very words of God, and the word of God specially sent to thee at this time: 'They shall never perish, neither shall any pluck them out of My hand.' Nay, nay, Odin cannot take a Christian soul to himself, even though he be sacrificed, martyred in his name," said Osric, consolingly.

"Then—then—I think I can forgive her; at least by and by," said Elswitha.

"The Lord Christ doth command thee to forgive her, even as He hath forgiven thee. Thou dost know that thou hast sinned against Him," said Osric.

"Yes, I have sinned, have grieved Him many times," said Elswitha sadly, and her thoughts went back to the murderous intent that had found a resting-place in her heart only a short time before.

They had drawn near the little hut or hermitage while they had been talking, and Osric left her with the herb-tea, while he went to ascertain if possible some particulars about the funeral of Thordstein. He would probably be able to hear this of some of the slaves, who would be sure to be loitering about at this time, while their masters were drinking; and they knew the monks well enough to trust them with any information they might be able to give, for they knew they were their friends.

So the first man Osric met he asked about this matter; but the man knew nothing, except that no funeral had been prepared, and so Thordstein would be buried under a heap of stones, instead of being burned.

Both modes were in use among the Danes, although, some years before, a warrior was almost invariably burned. If he were a chief, a hero, his warhorse, arms, gold and silver, and many of his most splendid trophies of victory, as well as whatever he held most dear, were placed with him on the pile.

Friends and relatives sometimes made it a point of honour to die with their leader, that his shade might be well attended in the halls of Odin. Nothing was more grand or noble to them than to enter Valhalla with a numerous retinue, all in costly armour or rich apparel. It was his knowledge of this custom, the fear that somebody was to be immolated as well as the dead man's horse, that he might be suitably attended, that induced Osric to persevere in his inquiries as to the sort of funeral Thordstein's was likely to be; for if there was to be anyone killed—unless they themselves wished it—he intended to call upon the thane to prevent it in the name of the king; for one of the terms of

SHADE: *ghost*
IMMOLATED: *sacrificed*

the contract upon which he held East Anglia as a fief of King Alfred was that it should be governed as a Christian kingdom.

It was, without doubt, this consideration that withheld the Danes from giving Thordstein such a grand funeral as he might otherwise have had, for he learned from another man soon after, that only his war-horse was to be slain, but most of his goods and movable possessions, as well as his arms, would be placed in the barrow or shallow grave with him. In this he saw that they utterly renounced Thorgiva, or they would have been left for her; but now they intended to act as though Thordstein had no wife, as though she were already dead.

He ventured to go as far as the deserted and desolate home of the husband and wife, so strangely separated; and if he had needed any confirmation of the enmity that now existed against Thorgiva, he saw it there.

By the light of the rising moon he could see that the door of the house was covered with writing, the letters or runes being all placed in a certain way, within certain lines, which it was believed gave them the magical effect of causing sickness and all kinds of misfortune to happen to the person against whom they were written.

Christian monk though he was, Osric could not help shuddering as he looked at the ominous characters with which the door was covered, for they were all noxious or "bitter runes," as they

FIEF: *territory*
ENMITY: *hostility*

were called, and he felt thankful now that Thorgiva could not come on a similar errand and see them for herself.

The night seemed suddenly to have grown colder after he had seen these magic runes, and he shivered again and again as he slowly retraced his steps homeward, and his teeth positively chattered when he went into the little refectory where his frugal meal of rye bread and water awaited him.

Brother Redwald was reading by the light of a flaring torch of pine-wood, and as Osric drew near he laid down the manuscript and held up the light, to look at him more closely. "Brother Osric, thou art ill," said Redwald, after looking at him for a minute or two.

"Nay, nay, it is but the chill evening air; 'tis autumn now, and the nights are growing cold," said Osric.

"Yes! cold and damp," said Redwald; "didst thou not see the mist rising from the water all around?"

"I did not notice it. I was full of thought, and—"

"It is not like thee, brother, not to see what I fear bodeth us no good," said Redwald, rather seriously.

Osric's thoughts flew at once to the magic "bitter runes," and he wondered whether the priest of Thor had dared to venture within their enclosure—had dared to write his mystic pagan letters upon any portion of the abbey or church or land that had been claimed in the names of the blessed

NOXIOUS: *harmful or hurtful*

saints, Peter and Paul—those first missionaries, who
had gone forth to carry the gospel of the grace of
God to Gentile sinners, pagans like these Danes.

But Redwald's next words dispelled this fear.
"The nights, as thou sayest, are very cold, and
the mist so heavy, that I fear this Ea is little better than a home for the bittern in the winter," he
said, speaking rather gloomily, and shivering as
he spoke.

Then for the first time Osric noticed that the
priest looked ill, and he said quickly, "Thou hast
been too careful about thy fishing, Redwald; thou
must not sit on the bank of the stream again, or
thou wilt be ill;" and then came the fear of the "bitter runes" again, and the effect they might have
upon his own comrades as well as upon Thorgiva.

Redwald would not admit that he had taken
cold while fishing. "It is the mist at night," he
said, "it wets our clothes, and we lie down in them
damp, and of course it finds its way through the
chinks of the walls, and keeps them damp all
night; mine were wet when I got up this morning,
and a house-carle told me today that nearly all the
Ea is a marsh, except during a dry summer, such
as this hath been."

Osric looked greatly perplexed when he heard
this, for what were they to do now? The summer
was almost at an end, the abbey and church were
more than half-built, and there were Thorgiva and
Elswitha upon their hands, so that they could not
leave this place. "A marsh, a swamp," he repeated

over and over again; and then he tried to recollect
all he had heard about the best way to drain wet
low-lying lands. They had taken advantage of the
rising ground, such as it was, and placed the abbey
and church on the top of it; and now it seemed
that they had better set about the work of draining it as fast as they could.

Redwald looked a little disappointed when Osric spoke of this to him. They had no right to throw
their lives away upon people who would never value the sacrifice; and their mission here was clearly
a failure, he thought, for what results could they
show for all their toil and labour?

Osric looked surprised, astonished; had they
not claimed all the land round about, in the names
of St. Peter and St. Paul? and had not the pagans
allowed the claim, and helped them to enclose
it—a Christian center in the midst of heatheness?
Was that nothing to rejoice over and thank God
for? Had they not been able to help the slaves too,
brought a ray of hope into their miserable lives?
and, in spite of the disappointments, had they not
good hope that paganism was losing its hold of
the Danes, and had they not one convert at least
from their midst in Thorgiva?

This was how Osric talked, bringing forth these
as well as other similar arguments to prove that if
they died this winter, their work here in East Anglia would not have been in vain, and that it was
clearly their duty to stand at their posts until they
died, if such was the will of God.

HEATHENESS: *heathen nations*

Chapter XI

Foes and Friends

VERY bravely and very hopefully did Osric talk
to Redwald and the other two brethren of
the certain success of their mission; but when they
had left him that night, and he was alone in his
cell, alone with his burden of care and fear and
dread, then it seemed that all his courage had forsaken him, and he bowed his head in his hands,
and tears of agony forced themselves from his
eyes. What should he, what ought he to do in this
strait? The other brethren had grown so disheart-
ened that they would be glad to return to their
own monastery, and leave the "filthy pagan crew"
to themselves; and whether he ought to oppose
this wish, or urge them to depart before the winter set in and made the roads impassable, was a
question he asked himself.

If the brethren wished so much to depart, it was
far better that they should do so—that Osric soon
decided; and he saw himself left alone in the half-
finished abbey, in the midst of these hostile hea-

thens, and shuddered as he thought of it. Then
came the recollection of the "bitter runes," and
he at once decided that his brethren were not so
much to blame after all. They could not help it. It
was the magical arts of the priest of Thor that had
worked this change in them, and it was better that
they should go at once, lest worse should happen
to them.

These considerations made Osric not only willing, but anxious, for his brethren to depart; but
he decided that they had better go to Thetford
first, and if possible remain there, at least until the
spring. He had no thought of leaving Ea himself.
He must not, dare not, forsake his chosen sphere
of labour; but who can wonder that his heart well-
nigh fainted at the prospect before him?

Sickness borne alone and unattended, want
of the barest necessaries of life, opposition from
fierce and cruel enemies, were not the only trials
or the worst that might await him, Osric thought,
for there were the "bitter runes" and all the magic
power that the priest of Thor was master of to be
conquered; and then he remembered the words he
had spoken when he first came to Ea, almost the
first he had uttered to these Danes. "The White
Christ hath a controversy with thy gods;" and as
he repeated the words again light broke in upon
his soul.

Surely the controversy was not his own, but
God's, and He would fight the battle for him. He

would not be left alone—he a simple unlearned monk, to contend against the power of these magical arts of the pagans, but God would fight for him. Then he recalled some of the loving, confident, trustful words of Elswitha, how she had spoken of God as being to her wise and strong and helpful as her father, gentle, tender and compassionate as her mother—how these dear parents had bade her look to Him as to father and mother combined, and how she had grown to think of Him and worship Him as her Father-God and Mother-God, because of His infinite compassion and love. The remembrance of these and similar words came to him now, and revived his drooping faith and courage. He too would try to look up to God, the great and mighty Jehovah, as being to him a Father-God too, although, strange as it may seem to us in these days, the world in that age but dimly comprehended this vital, essential relation that God bears to His creation.

We need to bear in mind that no single age possesses all the forms of truth: and that the gentleness and tenderness of God should be almost lost sight of when the belief in spiritual power and might was absolutely needed as a correlative in this age of brute force, when strength of muscle and sinew seemed the only thing to be proud of or gloried in, is not greatly to be wondered at.

It was because Elswitha in her dire need had learned to grasp this almost unknown side of the

CORRELATIVE: *balancing truth*

Divine character, that the monks had looked upon her as a saint; and Osric now, as he repeated the well-known words "Our Father," that had suddenly grown luminous with such deep meaning and comfort to his soul, almost feared lest he should be guilty of presumption in taking it to himself.

But he lay down to sleep at last, with the sweet words "Our Father" beating their refrain through his tired brain.

These four monks, living their almost solitary life here in Ea, rigidly kept to the rules of the monastery they had left, going through every service appointed for each day, and meeting in chapter for consultation each evening at the close of the day's work; and so it was not until they met again thus that Osric disclosed his plan of being left alone here in Ea.

His companions stood aghast when they heard it, and for a moment they repented of what they had said, and reproached themselves with being selfish and inconsiderate, and declared that they would not leave him; if he would not go with them, why, they would all stay and die together.

But Osric again shook his head. "Nay, nay; it is not our death that will profit these Danes: they need living men to teach them how to live without fighting and pillaging and ravaging their neighbours' homes—to teach them that the God Whose message to mankind is peace and goodwill is mightier than their slaughter-loving Odin;

and this I still hope to do by living here, my brethren, not dying—at least not yet," he added, with a smile.

They looked at each other and then at Osric, half-doubtingly. Surely he could not mean that he desired to live here. To die, and gain a martyr's crown in heaven, and the worship of men hereafter—that they could understand; but to live alone, uncared for, despised, and all but hated by those he sought to benefit—that they failed to comprehend, although they felt ashamed of their own selfishness in wishing to go away.

At length, however, Osric succeeded in convincing them that it was his wish more than their own that would take them away—that, as their leader, they were bound to obey him; and he bade them go to Thetford, and see how it fared with their brethren there, and if possible abide with them.

This compromise of the matter so far pleased his companions that they readily consented to adopt it, and also agreed to postpone their departure only until the next week; for the autumn was advancing now, and winter might be upon them before they were aware of it, and render traveling almost an impossibility.

But before the next week came, the incipient illness of Redwald had progressed so far that he was unable to leave his bed, and all the ingenuity and resources of the brethren had been taxed to render his cell more comfortable. The interstices

INCIPIENT: *beginning*
INTERSTICES: *narrow spaces*

between the ill-fitting timber walls—for they were
simply built of trees sawn down the middle—were
filled up with mud and dried moss, and some of
the wadmal given to them by King Guthrum, or
Æthelstan, was fastened over this for wall-riff; a
few wolf-skins had also been obtained from the
Danes, for the monks were ill-provided for such a
contingency as sickness.

The ague from which Redwald was suffering
might make it impossible for him to travel for several weeks, or even months, and so, after a few
days' delay, Osric persuaded the two others to
journey to Thetford by themselves, promising to
come thither himself with Redwald in the spring,
if only for a brief visit.

Thus urged, the two brethren wended their way
northward once more, feeling much less confident
than Osric that no evil would befall the brethren
they had left behind; nay, feeling very sad and ap-
prehensive now that Redwald had fallen sick.

Meanwhile Thorgiva had made some progress
towards recovery, although her grief for her husband's death greatly retarded it.

After Elswitha had assured her that every care
was being taken to give her husband a funeral
worthy of a hero and a warrior, she seemed to
take very little notice of her nurse for some days.
She allowed her to nurse the baby when he grew
tired of lying in bed by her side, and took the food
and medicine that she brought to her; but the two

AGUE: *a disease marked by fits of chills, fever and sweating;
probably malaria*

women rarely spoke, and at last Elswitha grew ac-
customed to the presence of her dreaded enemy,
and felt some pity for her in her silent unobtrusive
sorrow. She would not have ventured to give ex-
pression to this, however; to dare to pity a Danish woman, and such a woman as Thorgiva, might
cost her her life even here.

She had seen no evidence as yet of her being a
Christian, for her silent endurance was only the
result of the fortitude in which every child was
trained—a submission to the inevitable with calm-
ness when it was useless to struggle against it.

But when she had been there above a week, and
the body of Thordstein had been laid in its hon-
oured grave, she suddenly said to Elswitha one
day, "The monk said thou wert a Christian."

Elswitha started, and her pale face flushed. "Yes,
I am a Christian," she said, falteringly.

"Then why dost thou not pray to thy God? I have
been here some days, and waited and watched for
thee to kneel down, as Osric did when he came to
visit my Thordstein."

Elswitha hung her head. "I was afraid," she said
humbly, "and went out into the wood to pray."

"Afraid!" uttered Thorgiva, looking curiously at
the girl; and then for the first time she recognized
her, and started up in bed with the shock of surprise. "Thou—thou art Elswitha, who was devoted
to Odin; whom I devoted to our war-god!" she exclaimed.

But the moment Elswitha heard these words, instead of being overcome with alarm and terror, as she had feared, she said calmly, "Yes; I am Elswitha; the Lord Christ hath rescued me from Odin and"—"from thee" she was about to add, but before she could say this, Thorgiva had fallen back upon the bed fainting.

Elswitha raised Thorgiva's head upon her arm, and as she sprinkled her face with water, she wondered why she dared to do it—why she was not still afraid to approach too near. Never in her wildest imaginings could she have thought it possible that she should ever hold Thorgiva, as she now did, helpless almost as an infant—entirely in her power now, if she wished to kill her. Kill her? Elswitha shrank with horror at the recollection of the thought, and, as if she might make reparation for even the remembrance, she bent her head and kissed the pale inanimate face.

But Thorgiva was conscious of the unwonted action, and as she opened her eyes Elswitha's face grew rosy, and she expected to see her patient start away from her in indignation and disgust. But, to her surprise, Thorgiva said rather faintly, "Canst thou forgive me, Elswitha?"

But the girl could not answer, for the profound astonishment she felt at the question. Could it be the proud, fierce Thorgiva asking forgiveness? and of her?

Before she answered, or could recover from her

REPARATION: *amends*
UNWONTED: *unusual*

astonishment sufficiently to speak, Thorgiva said, "Thou hast much to forgive, Elswitha, for I robbed thee of father and mother, to devote them to Odin; and how thou didst thyself escape, when I would afterwards have given thee, hath ever been a puzzle I could not comprehend, unless thou didst use magical arts to aid thee."

Elswitha shook her head. "Nay, I did but pray to God, my Father in heaven, and He sent His servants to deliver me."

"It was about the time that the monks came; didst thou know they were coming?"

"Nay, I never expected any Christian monks would be bold enough to come to Ea; but I thought— I knew—that my God was greater than Odin or Thor, and could deliver me out of their hands."

"Thou dost believe in thy White Christ, Elswitha, although I often told thee He was but a poor pitiful God?"

"Nay, not poor, but rich in mercy and tenderness to all who need it," said Elswitha.

"Thou art a brave girl too, although I thought thee only a miserable Angle, not worthy the consideration of a Dane."

"Nay, I am not brave," dissented Elswitha; "I am weak and cowardly, or—or I should not have been afraid of thee—afraid to kneel down and pray where thou couldst see me."

"But thou wilt not be afraid now; thou wilt kneel down and pray for me to thy God."

And Elswitha kneeled down; and from that time the dread terror of Thorgiva's presence left her, and at last she began to feel glad that Osric had brought her, for Thorgiva's child was a boundless source of interest to her, and she soon grew to love him so much that she could not endure the thought of parting with him.

At first Thorgiva seemed inclined to be jealous of Elswitha's love for her little one, and of the child's partiality for his gentle nurse; but after a time this feeling was conquered, and one day she said to Elswitha, "Thou shalt teach my little Aethelstan to know thy God, for I—I shall never be more than half a Christian, even though I be baptized; for I can never forget Odin and Thor, and it doth always seem to me that thy God is but a little stronger than they."

Doubtless the old pagan belief would cling to her more or less to the very end of her life; but Thorgiva's faith, and with it her whole character, had undergone a wonderful change. Old things had passed away, for she no longer despised the mercy and love that was offered her, although it was some time before she could believe that such a great sinner as she had been could be pardoned, that such sins as hers could be washed away, even in the blood of Christ.

That Elswitha could forgive all that she had suffered at her hands—could forgive her murder of father and mother, and all the persecutions she had inflicted because of her religion, helped her to believe at last that God too might forgive her, although her sins against Him were tenfold more than those against Elswitha.

But perhaps of all the means that God used to bring this fierce, proud, haughty woman to Himself, her baby was the most powerful. Her love for her child was deep and strong, and through this deep, strong, earnest love, she came at last to understand something of that love of God which she had so often despised, as she had contemned this mother-love before it came to her. Now she knew that it was stronger than pride, for she would have bowed herself in the dust to save her child; she felt grateful and thankful to her former slave Elswitha, whom she had so much despised, because she was kind to the little one.

CONTEMNED: *despised, scorned*

Chapter XII

The Hymns of Cædmon

HOW much our little band of Christians owed to the presence of a babe among them, during the dreary winter that followed, none perhaps but God knew. Living, or rather starving, in that little timber hut in the forest was very different from life in the village of Ea, where, if it was rough and coarse, there was always plenty to eat and drink. Pork and ale, if not as plentiful as in the halls of Odin, seldom ran short, and feasting and sports were the order of the day during the long severe frosts of this season. Wrestling-matches, hunting the wild boars and wolves in the forests, varied by the periodical feasts of their gods, and listening to the minstrel or gleeman in the mead-hall of their chief, served to pass the time away that would otherwise have hung heavy on their hands in their own dull houses. The women could not of course join in the wrestling, but they were always present to witness it, and exercised their younger children in running, leaping, and jumping, as well

as encouraged their husbands, brothers, and lovers in their various feats of agility and strength. A
young Dane knew it would be useless to aspire to
the hand, or even gain an approving smile, from
any girl unless he had first proved himself worthy
to become a warrior, and for this he was willing to
endure hunger, cold, pain and weariness; for what
glory could be greater than that of being a warrior and winning the heart of some true Danish
woman brave as himself—a very lioness to her foes,
but gentle as a lamb to him?

Such a woman as this was Thorgiva, and many
had been the wrestling-matches and all but mortal
combats for the honour of winning a smile from
her; and no trial of arms was considered of much
importance if she were not there to cheer the conqueror at the critical moment, and help him to
win the victory.

This had been Thorgiva's world, and this she
had had to renounce on becoming a Christian; and
it was no slight test of her principles, this dreary
winter, to be shut up in that log hut, often lying in
trembling agony lest some hungry wolf, which they
could hear prowling about in the neighbourhood,
should burst in upon them and tear the babe from
her arms. It was harder too to bear hunger, when
she knew that want of food for herself meant lack
of nourishment for her darling; and yet, had it not
been for the child, she would have felt ready to lie
down and die rather than eat the poor, meager

fare that Elswitha was able to provide. It was not much pork or beef that ever found its way to them now, although they had by far the larger share of the presents occasionally made to Osric by her countrymen. At the beginning of the winter they had a little flour and oatmeal and a few vegetables, and with these Elswitha contrived to pound up a few acorns and wild nuts, and roots were boiled to make soup with the vegetables; and so they eked out a subsistence from day to day.

They both grew thin and wan, and baby did not thrive so well as when food was more plentiful; but to Elswitha this life of peace, with the baby to nurse and watch and talk to, was as heaven to what she had previously endured, and so she was invariably cheerful and happy, and ever ready to talk of the goodness and love of her Father in heaven, whenever Thorgiva would listen.

Among the Danes their scalds or bards were held in as high estimation as the minstrels or gleemen among the Anglo-Saxons, and one day Elswitha told Thorgiva of their wonderful poet Cædmon, and of his miraculous gift, as all the monks and learned men of his day declared it to be.

"Why, what dost thou mean, Elswitha?" said Thorgiva, who was always ready to listen to any story of the marvelous.

Thus encouraged the girl soon began her tale. "The harp was often passed to Cædmon in the mead-hall, but he could never sing, as could all the

SCALDS OR BARDS: *traveling poets*

other lithsmen and house-carles, and right sorely
it grieved him that he had to pass it on in silence to
his neighbour. One day when it came to his turn,
and he had to pass the harp as usual, he was so
overcome with grief and shame that he went out at
once to the barn, with the excuse that he was going to feed the cattle; but when he got there he fell
on his face and prayed to God to help him to sing
like the others, and that very night God put the
song of the Creation into his heart." And Elswitha
sang to Thorgiva the hymn Osric had heard her
singing in the forest.

"And what befell him next? Did he sing other
songs? Dost thou know any more?" asked Thorgiva, eagerly.

"Oh yes; the reeve of the village heard him sing
this first song, and went to the monastery and told
the monks about it, and they sent for Cædmon to
come and live with them and make other songs,
that they might write them from his mouth—for
Cædmon could neither read nor write; and so the
monks would read to him parts of the Scripture—
the Word of God—and he would tune it into most
marvelous sweet poesy, such as the world hath
never seen before."

Of course Elswitha's world was not a very wide
one, and as Cædmon was the earliest Anglo-Saxon
poet of whom we have any record, his gift of song
would be the wonder of the age in which he lived.
"Dost thou know anything—any other saga, like

REEVE: *an Anglo-Saxon official appointed by the king*
POESY: *poetry*

unto that thou hast now sung?" asked Thorgiva; for this hymn of Cædmon's reminded her of their own sagas as sung by their scalds.

"Yes, I can sing one of the Deluge," said Elswitha; and settling the baby on her lap, she sang in a low recitative tone:—

"The Lord sent rain from heaven, and o'er the land
Wide wasting bade the whelming torrents rush.
Dark from the abyss, with hideous roar, burst forth
The imprisoned waters. Ocean heaved his tide
High o'er his wonted limits; strong was he
And mighty in his wrath, that on the plains
Poured that avenging stream, and swept to death,
Wide through the realms of earth, a sinful race.
Now o'er each dwelling-place of man the wave
Spread desolation, for the Lord fulfilled
His anger upon mortals: forty days
And forty nights continuous that dark flood,
Fear-struck and fainting, drove them to their doom.
Vengeance and death in all their terror raged.
The heaven-commissioned waters on all flesh
Worked the dread punishment of lawless lust.
Fearful and wild, wherever beneath the sky
Earth spreads her ample confines,
O'er-towered the mountains; and secure meanwhile,
With all her inmates, rose the sacred bark,
Sped by the power that made creation rise.
So swelled the flood, that soon its buoyant load
The watery waste encompassed; fearless then
Of hunger or of harm, they rode at large
Beneath heaven's canopy; the billows' rage
Touched not that fated vessel, for their Lord
Was with them still, the Holy One preserved them.
Full fifteen cubits o'er the mountain heights
The sea flood rose, and drank the force of man.

DELUGE: *the great flood of Noah's time*
WONTED: *usual*

> Wondrous and awful was that waste of waters.
> They were cut off from men, and none was near them,
> Save Him that reigns above; all else on earth
> The whelming host of waters covered wide:
> That ark alone the Almighty One upheld."

Thorgiva was not the only listener, for Osric had entered while Elswitha was singing, and when she would have stopped he said, "Go on, go on; I would fain hear it all."

As she finished there was a silence for a few minutes, and then the monk said, turning to Thorgiva, "Dost thou not think thy people would listen to such a hymn as that?"

"Yes! 'tis more marvelous than our own sagas; and if one would sing it to the freemen when they are gathered in the mead-hall of our thane, or to the house-carles, it would teach them that thy God is a God greater than even Odin, though He be a God of love and mercy."

"Yes, the wondrous hymn sings of mercy," said Elswitha; "the Almighty One, our Father, upheld the ark and guided it aright."

"And it tells of a might greater than Thor's, or of Njörd's, thy god of winds and waters," said Osric.

"Yes, it is as the mighty God thou must first speak of Him to our Dane-folk," said Thorgiva, with a sigh.

"And they will listen to these songs of holy Cædmon, as they listen to the scalds and their sagas," said Osric, confidently.

"Yes! an thou couldst sing them such sagas as these," replied the woman.

"I will sing them: Elswitha hath reminded me of what I had well-nigh forgotten," said the monk, eagerly; "thou shalt help me to remember these songs of Cædmon."

But poor Elswitha, who had no idea of the reverence with which she was viewed by the monks, looked almost aghast at the approving words. "I—I should be afraid to teach one so wise as thou art," she said, simply.

"Nay, my daughter, but thou hast already taught me many things; and I would thou shouldst help me bring to mind these songs again; for although Redwald is learned in the arts of reading and writing, they are of little use among the Dane-folk; but these sagas they would listen to, I trow."

And Osric sat down on one of the logs that served for seats, and Elswitha repeated over the first lines of "The Deluge."

He had learned it at the monastery long ago, but it had almost slipped from his memory, until he heard Elswitha repeating it; but the familiar words were soon recalled now, and he went back to his companion with a new power and fresh hope.

Redwald was still weak and ailing, and the ague did not seem to leave him entirely, although he was much better.

He had never been out beyond the stockade that enclosed their own ground since the departure of the other brethren. He often thought he should not live to see the church and abbey completed; for it was sometimes more than his feeble strength could bear to read the appointed prayers every day.

Osric did everything possible, not merely to do him good, but to relieve the tedium of his wearisome illness, and it was with eager, bounding steps that he went home today to impart what he knew of Cædmon's poetry.

Anything that could break the dreary monotony of the empty hours was welcome to Redwald now; and to learn some of the great poet's words was to him a pleasure as great as it was unexpected, and he saw now an opportunity of greater usefulness, if he should ever get well again, so as to be able to go out; for he had heard of a certain bishop who did not think any work too lowly, if only he might win some to the knowledge of God, who had stood at the end of a bridge where people were frequently passing, and there sang the songs of Cædmon to many who stopped to listen to the sweet heavenly words.

He quickly mastered the lines Osric had learned, for he too had heard them before; and now, to preserve them more surely, he not only committed them to memory but wrote them out on a piece of parchment afterwards.

So Elswitha the slave became a teacher of the monks as well as a nurse to Thorgiva and her baby.

But Osric was not content with merely teaching Redwald what he had learned, but was anxious to improve this winter season by teaching some of the Dane-folk also; for as soon as spring should come again the old restless longing to be going on some campaign would seize them as usual, and they would be too irritable and impatient to listen to anything but orders to arm and march forward to the fight. Now if he could only gain admission to the mead-hall of the thane, when there was a gathering of the lithsmen and freemen of the village, they might listen to these songs; more especially as he could play a little on the harp, like their own scalds.

So he watched his opportunity, and the next time there was a gathering of the Dane-folk he went up the hill to the mead-hall, and went in with the rest, as though he had been a traveler on his journey, and passing that way. The men looked at each other as he came among them, but it was scarcely from the cause that Osric supposed, for they were wondering whether it was himself or some other monk, who had been half-starved on his journey, so wan and thin and worn did he look.

The fact was, Osric had fared worse than any of his companions this winter; for Redwald had been almost his first care, and when Redwald's wants had been supplied, Thorgiva and Elswitha needed all the meat and most nourishing food he could get for them; so that his own share of this had been very small indeed, and he had lived upon the poorest and meanest fare himself.

It was owing to this fact, perhaps, that the monk had such a cordial reception accorded him, for his pale, pinched, yet bright and cheerful face appealed to these Danes more powerfully than anything else. He bore the marks of suffering patiently endured. He was a brave man, and the Danes could recognize and honour bravery wherever they saw it; and they immediately invited him to the feast that was being prepared, and the savoury smell of which even now filled the hall. But, hungry as he was, and thankful as he would have been for one full meal at this time, he knew that the huge joints of beef and pork had been offered in sacrifice to their gods, the blood being sprinkled on the altar and the entrails critically examined by the priest, to ascertain what events were likely to befall them during the coming year, while the remainder of the carcass was to be consumed by the worshipers in honour of the god.

To partake therefore of this feast, he felt would be to become an idolater, and, hungry as he might be, the feast could not be touched by Osric.

"I came not for this feast, but—"

"But thou dost look as though a good meal would do thee no harm," interrupted one of the men.

"Doubtless we all know what hunger is sometimes," said the monk, trying to speak lightly; but he did wish the smell of the meat was not so appetizing, for it certainly increased his craving for food.

He resolved to get away if possible before the feast was served, and so, asking for the loan of a harp, as he did not possess one of his own, he soon began Cædmon's song of the Deluge, the Danes listening with deep attention.

"It is a true song—grand as our own sagas," remarked one, as Osric concluded his singing.

"And dost thou mean to say that thy God, the mean pitiful God of these conquered Angles, could make the great sea roll its waves over all the land until the very mountains were covered?"

"Nay, nay; say not that such a God is mean and pitiful," interrupted another Dane, before Osric could reply. "Who among our sons of Odin could match such a deed as this?" he added.

"Monk, is thy saga true?" asked another, in an awestruck whisper.

"Yes! as true as that there is a sun in the heavens is this saga of the Deluge," said Osric, solemnly lifting his hand.

"And all men upon the earth were swept to death by this waste of water?" said another.

"How then canst thou say thy God is merciful, monk?" asked a third.

"Was He not merciful and tender to those who, believing the warning He had given, betook themselves to the refuge He had provided—

"Secure meanwhile,
With all her inmates, rose the sacred bark,
Sped by the power that bade creation rise.
They were cut off from men, and none was near them,
Save Him that reigns above."

Osric repeated the words slowly, and then asked, "Does not the saga tell of mercy as well as punishment?"

"And how many were there in this mighty, magic ship?" asked one.

"Only eight," replied Osric.

"Only eight! thy God would think eight men, out of thousands, worth saving!"

"If there had been but one, God would think him worth saving," said Osric. And with this for a text he went on to declare to them once more the message God had sent to them by his mouth.

There was no noisy brawling or contending now, but they listened as they had never listened before; and when he left off speaking, as they began to bring in the huge lumps of meat on spits, they again pressed him to partake of their feast.

"Nay, nay, but thou knowest I have already said I may not; my God hath forbidden things offered first unto idols."

"But thou art hungry," said one.

"That is no new thing, but 'tis better to deny the stomach than disobey God." And, lest the sight and smell of all this good food should prove too strong a temptation, Osric hurried from the hall as fast as his now enfeebled strength would permit.

Chapter XIII

The Priest of Thor

TO say that Osric's abrupt departure created surprise among the Danes would not express a tithe of the astonishment they felt as they watched him leave the hall.

The monk was hungry—almost dying for want of food, and there was the smoking savoury meat offered to him; and yet he refused it, because it was part of their sacrifice, and therefore forbidden by God!

"But his God is merciful; He is not like Thor, delighting in slaughter and vengeance," said one; "He saved those men in the magic ship, when all else was swept away; surely He would not kill this monk for tasting food when he was starving, even though it had been forbidden."

It was clearly a matter they could not understand—a riddle they could not solve; for only the terror of their Thunderer's vengeance would have deterred them from partaking of such a feast, even though it had been ten times forbidden.

TITHE: *tenth*

This act of Osric's made as great an impression upon their minds as the saga he had sung to them, and before the feast was over it had been decided that another bullock should be killed the next day, and half of it carried to the abbey; for they had little doubt but that all the companions of the monk were almost as badly fed.

The priest of Thor had promised them that all the monks should leave Ea before this time; they would never be able to stand out against the powerful charms he had used, the "bitter runes" that had been written against them, he said, and he had put himself into a violent passion when he saw Osric approaching the mead-hall, and vowed that he should not escape the power of his magic this time, he should not leave the hall alive. The Danes laughed at his anger, and were quite willing to see him exercise his boasted power. Of late they had begun to doubt, for Thorgiva had not been carried off to Niflheim, as he said she had: one or two had seen her go into a little hut in the forest, which the monks had doubtless built for her. They had never happened to catch a glimpse of Elswitha, and supposed that Thorgiva lived there alone with her child. They had kept a pretty strict watch upon the movements of the monks, although they had seemed to have forgotten their existence.

The Danes knew that two of the brethren had left, and had watched for Osric and Redwald to follow them, or die, according to their priest's prediction; but, although Redwald had been very ill, as all strangers were the first winter they lived in their swampy island, he showed no symptoms of dying, but, on the contrary, they had seen him walking about, whenever there was a gleam of sunshine to tempt him out. It was clear too that, in spite of all the discouragements they had met with, these monks did not intend to give up their residence on the island, for whenever the weather would permit Osric had been busy digging trenches and draining the land round about the abbey; and therefore they might as well be on good terms with their uninvited guests, since the priest could not get rid of them.

So the next morning Osric's heart was gladdened with the sight of half a bullock being laid down at the door of their dwelling by two stout house-carles, who brought a message from the thane that they were to hold a feast to their God by themselves, since they would not share in theirs. And Osric sent back a message of thanks, and also a request that he might come to the mead-hall again, and sing them another saga; for Elswitha had begun to teach him Cædmon's song of "The Overthrow of the Egyptians," which he knew would stir the hearts of these Danes.

When the messengers had departed, Osric shed tears of thankful joy over the huge joints of meat that would be of so much service to them. They all needed good nourishing food now, and none more so than himself; and yet if only a small quantity had been sent, he would have felt it to be his duty to share it between the others alone.

Now, however, they had a store that would give them a feast for many days to come; and so, cutting a piece off for themselves, he left Redwald to cook it, while he carried some to Thorgiva without delay. He little guessed that he was being watched by two pairs of stealthy eyes, each intent upon discovering Thorgiva's hiding-place, but neither knowing that the other was watching, until they emerged from behind some trees face to face soon after Osric had passed.

It was the priest of Thor and the widow's brother, and the two men glared at each other with a look of deadly hatred.

"Thou sayest thy bitter runes hath sent my sister to Niflheim," said the Dane, speaking in a whisper.

"I say, if the magic runes hath failed, this spear shall do their work," said the priest, in a hissing tone of suppressed rage.

In a moment the gigantic Dane had seized him by the throat, and hurled him to the ground.

"Thou wilt kill Thorgiva with this spear, since thy magic hath failed?" he said, wresting the weapon from the priest's hand, and loosening his grip upon his throat.

"Is she not a Christian? Hath she not denied our mighty Odin? And dost thou not hate her for

THE TWO MEN GLARED AT EACH OTHER

dishonouring the name of thy ancestors?" panted the priest.

"Nay, I do not hate her. Thou didst rouse my anger against her, so that I would have killed her, to send her soul to Odin; but when thou didst tell me she should go to the dread Niflheim, then my anger died, and I remembered she was my sister, the noblest woman in Ea." And the grip once more tightened on the priest's throat, and his face turned a livid hue under the choking pressure.

But the Dane did not mean to kill him; he relaxed his hold upon his throat the next minute, and once more spoke to him: "Thou dost hate my sister because she, the noblest woman amongst us, hath forsaken the old gods; and thou dost think that now we have so little faith in thee or the old religion, except as it doth serve our own purposes, we too shall turn to this God, and therefore thou wouldst kill her."

"Yes," admitted the priest.

"Yes! thou dost accuse her of forswearing the religion of our ancestors; but what of thee, thou defiled priest? Art thou worthy to draw near to the altar again, when thou hast come forth armed with that?" and he pointed to the spear that lay near them.

"I—I know it is forbidden us to bear arms, but—"

"But revenge is more to thee than obedience to thy god; therefore thou canst have but little faith or fear in our slaughter-loving Odin," interrupted the Dane. "Dost thou remember the monk yesterday? He came to the feast famishing with hunger, but not the sight or smell of our savoury meats could tempt him to eat what his God had forbidden." He went on, "He believed in his God, and I believe in Him too. Dost thou hear, priest? If there is a God in the universe, it is the God of the Christians, and Thorgiva will not long be the only Christian among the Danes of Ea."

"Nay, nay; say not thou wilt forsake thy war-god, thou wilt—"

"I say *thy* work among us is over, and thou must depart from Ea," interrupted his adversary; "dost thou think we will have a defiled priest to offer our sacrifices?" he demanded.

The priest wished most heartily that he could have contented himself without interfering with Thorgiva, or had thrown the spear away when he found he was not alone in the forest; for he knew the temper of the man with whom he had to deal, and was assured that he would not brook any delay, and that nothing would be gained now by trying to stay in the village; every man and woman among them would know he was virtually an apostate from the old religion, and they were too proud and haughty to suffer a defiled priest to offer sacrifices for them.

So, after a few minutes' consideration of these points, he resolved to yield, and gave the required promise to leave Ea at once. The Dane watched

BROOK: *stand for, tolerate*
APOSTATE: *someone who has abandoned his religion*

the priest for a few minutes as he hastened down the path towards the village. He then went on in the direction taken by Osric, hoping to find the hut that had been described to him.

He had not gone far before he came to the stockade which enclosed the abbey land, and it was within this he had heard that his sister had found a refuge. He only wanted to see for himself that she was safe and well, or he would not otherwise have ventured to set his foot upon the ground that had been claimed for this great God and His earls St. Peter and St. Paul, whoever they might be. For in his newborn reverence and awe he would not have dared to bring spear and battle-axe there, lest this mighty God, who had rolled the ocean over the land, should instantly take vengeance upon him.

Even now, peaceful as his errand was, he almost trembled with misgiving lest he should incur the anger of God, as he drew near the hermitage, to which the sound of voices had directed his steps. He thought he could discern Thorgiva's as he drew nearer, and making a slight detour, he went round to the back of the hut, stealing softly to the further side, where, through a crevice in the wall, he could see and hear all that went on inside.

He was somewhat startled to see another woman there besides Thorgiva; but he was too anxious to see how his sister was looking to pay much heed to Elswitha, who was busy with the meat Osric had brought, cutting some of it up to make a savoury soup.

The monk rose to leave a minute or two after he got there, and the Dane watched him depart, resolving to wait a little while and see something more of his sister.

When the meat was cut up, and placed in the pot to boil, Elswitha turned to take the baby; but Thorgiva kept him in her arms.

"I want thee to sing the saga to me thou hast been teaching to father Osric," she said.

And Elswitha sat down on the ground at her feet, and sang in a clear sweet voice:—

> "The heathen stood aghast; fierce raged the flood,
> And wailing spirits gave the shriek of death.
> The blood streamed fresh on each man's destined grave,
> The sea foamed gore; screams were amid the waves,
> As though the waters wept; darkling uprose
> The whirlpool mists. Egypt was backward turned;
> Dismayed they fled; fear struck their inmost souls.
> How fallen their boasting now! How would they joy
> Once more to reach their home! But that foul surf,
> Swift rolling in its power, o'erwhelmed their pride."

At this point the baby cried, and interrupted the singing, and the listener outside crept away, wondering where he had seen Elswitha before, and how his sister could endure this banishment from all the pleasures and excitements of their feasts and wrestling-matches, and yet look so peaceful and contented as she did.

True, her loneliness might be cheered a little by hearing such wonderful sagas as these sung; and truly this God they told of must be a mighty God; but whoever heard of a Danish woman voluntarily banishing herself from all the pleasures of life and the society of friends, for the sake of religion—because she would not give up the worship of a particular god?

The idea would have been simply ridiculous; but the fact could not be denied that Thorgiva, the proudest and most heroic of their women, had done this, and persisted in doing it.

All these thoughts passed through her brother's mind as he slowly took his way homeward, resolving to keep his own counsel for the present about the encounter with the priest of Thor, if he had left the village by the time he returned. If not—if he failed to keep his promise—he would denounce him at once as unfit to hold the sacred office, because he had defiled himself by bearing arms. And, lax as these Danes might be in their own faith and practice of religion, they were not men to put up with laxity in those whom they paid to serve and appease the gods for them.

This the priest of Thor knew, and, aware of the slight hold paganism now had upon the people, he was not one to risk his personal safety for the sake of a religion he had less faith in than his followers. And so, before Thorgiva's brother, Lodbrog, had reached the village, the priest had left it.

LAXITY: *carelessness*
APPEASE: *satisfy the demands of*

Lodbrog went quietly to his own home, saying nothing of what had happened until the next day, when some of the first who went out came running back to give the alarm that the sacred fire was no longer burning on the altar of Thor.

Many trembled when they heard it, fearing the vengeance of their terrible god, and wondering who had been so bold as to dare to extinguish this flame. Suspicion pointed to the monks; for no Dane would risk an approach to the altar of their fierce war-god, and the rumour soon spread through the village that Osric had done it during the night.

Lodbrog heard the rumour, and shook his head, but would not contradict it at once. "If the monks have done this in the night, where is the priest this morning? Why did he not kindle the fire again at the dawn of day?" he said.

Then there was a search for the priest; but he could not be found, and no one else dared to go near the altar. After they had searched in vain for the priest for several hours, and Lodbrog saw that a notion was arising that this mysterious disappearance was likewise owing to Osric, he told them of his encounter in the forest the day before, and how the priest had defiled himself by bearing arms for the sake of wreaking his vengence on Thorgiva.

The tide of popular feeling, so strong against the widow at the time of her husband's death, had been gradually changing of late, and now, at the words "vengeance being wreaked upon her," they forgot her offense in the full tide of their sympathy on her behalf.

"Who shall dare to take vengeance upon Dane-folk, even though they do choose to serve another God? Are we not a fierce people? Are we not all Vikings, and the sons and daughters of Vikings? If our gods be offended, let them avenge themselves upon us; but let not a priest try to take vengeance."

A ringing cheer greeted this speech, and it was plain that the people were in no temper to be coerced in the matter of their religion. They would be free in this, as in all else, free to choose whom they would serve among their own or the gods of other nations; even as they were free to serve whom they would among the kings and rulers of the world. This was their bold declaration, and later in the day Osric was sent for to the mead-hall again, to tell them something of the conditions upon which they might expect that the God of the Christians would become their God.

Osric took this opportunity of singing Cædmon's hymn, of "The Overthrow of the Egyptians" and "The Deliverance of Israel," which of course increased their desire to call this mighty God their God; but they were disappointed at the terms upon which He would receive them to be His people.

They must be merciful, peaceable and honest, Osric declared; but the Danes shook their heads. The terms were too hard. They could not give up their love of revenge and war and pillage. They were sorry this God of the Christians would not take them upon any other condition; for they had little or no faith in their old gods now.

This was what they told Osric; but at the same time they intimated that they should always be glad to hear him sing the wonderful sagas that told of his God. And the monk, thankful for even this small encouragement, returned home to tell his companion that the Danes were not far from the kingdom of heaven.

INTIMATED: *hinted*

Chapter XIV

The Secret of Eglesdune

THE dull dreary days of winter passed away at last, and Osric, as he looked at the forsaken altar of Thor, where no fire had been burning now for some weeks, lifted his heart in thankfulness to God; for surely the wintry season of opposition and reproach was passing too, and God was touching the hearts of these Danes. There was a stirring of life among these dry branches, as among the trees of the forest, and they too would bud and blossom and bring forth fruit, so that East Anglia should again be a Christian kingdom, not merely by charter with King Alfred, but by the people's will and choice.

Redwald was almost well again now, and, like Osric, had renewed his faith and courage by the hopeful signs around, and one of the most hopeful was that two or three came to ask how they should set about draining and planting their land, that they might sow and reap for themselves.

Osric's heart almost stood still with thankfulness and joy when he heard this request. If they could only be induced to cultivate the land, instead of spending all their time in martial exercises and moaning over the number of white shields there were among them, it would be better than all the stockades and earthworks for the protection of Mercia and Wessex; and if one or two would only be brave enough to set the example, there would soon be others willing to follow.

Lodbrog was one who had come to ask the advice of Osric about his land; and as the monk walked through the village with him, to see the plot of ground he proposed to plant, he told the monk that the piece adjoining his own had belonged to Thordstein, and that it would be well for Thorgiva to claim it for her child without delay.

"Hast thou seen Thorgiva?" asked Osric, in some surprise.

"Many among us have caught a glimpse of her while in the forest hunting," said her brother, somewhat evasively.

"And thou dost think her claim for this land will be allowed?" said Osric.

"Who can gainsay it? Nay, the Dane-folk will be glad to see her again; and her house doth still wait for her."

"But—but dost thou not know that thy sister is a Christian—that she is to be baptized as soon as may be?" said Osric.

"And I—I am almost a Christian," said Lodbrog, in a lower tone. "The fire of Thor will never be lighted again, I trow; and we have no priest among us to stir up our zeal for the gods and hatred of our fellows. Tell Thorgiva that Lodbrog doth bid her come home; and as a proof of my sincerity, she may tell thee the secret of Eglesdune."

Osric did not trouble his mind much about what the "secret of Eglesdune" might be, in the interest of advising Lodbrog as to the best way of improving his land. But when he had done this, and the men had begun the work of digging, he resolved to go and tell Thorgiva what her brother had said.

She started and turned deathly pale, as he said, "Thou wilt tell me this secret of Eglesdune."

"I have long wished to tell thee; but I dared not, for fear thou shouldst betray it; for I knew that thou couldst not keep it to thyself," said Thorgiva, with trembling lips.

"Nay! but if it would have relieved thee to confess this thing to me before, thou knowest I dared not tell it to any but God."

"Ah! thou knowest not what thou sayest! Didst thou ever hear where King Edmund was slain?" asked Thorgiva.

Osric started at the question, but Elswitha said in a whisper, "It was close to Eglesdune, for my father hath shown me the place where they found his head, which the Danes cut off and threw into the thickest part of the forest. He was one of those who went in search of it, who saw the wolf holding the sacred relic between his paws."

But Osric had never heard this marvelous tale concerning the saint-king; and so Elswitha told it, as she had heard it from her father and mother a few years before.

The Danes having slain the king and his faithful friend, Bishop Humbert, and driven all the Angles whom they did not slaughter away from Eglesdune, soon grew tired of the place themselves, and left; when the Angles ventured to creep from their hiding-places and come back, and their first care was to search for the body of King Edmund. This was soon found, but the head was nowhere to be seen; and at last it was agreed that they should divide themselves into parties and explore the adjacent wood. Here some of them, being separated from their companions, called out, "Where are you?" A voice answered, "Here, here, here;" but on reaching the spot, instead of seeing their friends, there lay the head, and a wolf stood guarding it. He allowed them to take it up from the ground, but followed them, and watched them place it on the neck of the body, to which it was instantly joined. After this miracle the body was reverently buried, and the Angles began to build a little timber church over the grave; but before it could be finished, the Danes came and drove us all away, and the chapel was thrown down."

This was Elswitha's story, and of course Osric believed every word. It was no more than might be expected, that a miracle of some sort should be performed. An age so superstitious and credulous is sure to abound in miracles, and this of King Edmund's head was not more extraordinary than many others currently believed.

So no question of its authenticity ever crossed Osric's mind; his only anxiety was to know whether the spot could be identified where his body had been laid.

Elswitha shook her head. She was not sure whether she could remember this; it was so long since she had left Eglesdune: she only knew that the way to it lay through this forest, and she was trying to find her way thither when met by the monks.

Thorgiva, however, could supply this information, although the Danes had since burned the church, that the name of the hero-king might be forgotten and his few remaining Angle subjects deterred from following the religion of their fathers. This was the secret of Eglesdune; for Thorgiva's family had not only taken an active part in the death of the king, but had since tried to stamp out all remembrance of him from the earth, and so his grave, the precise spot where his body actually lay, was known only to Lodbrog, Thordstein and Thorgiva.

That her brother would ever voluntarily disclose

CREDULOUS: *overly willing to believe or trust*

this secret she had never once thought possible, although the possession of it had weighed upon her own mind lately, and often made her very unhappy.

She was willing enough to accompany the monk to Eglesdune, and point out the spot where the royal martyr had been buried. It was about three miles and a half from Ea, on the road to Thetford, and it was agreed that they should go the following day, and that Elswitha should accompany them, to share in the task of carrying the little Æthelstan.

Eglesdune had been the home of Elswitha before the Danes came and carried her away captive; and her heart beat high with hope now, at the thought of going back to the old familiar scenes of her childhood; for she might see friends again after all—friends of her own kindred, for many had made good their escape when she and her parents were brought captive to Ea, and she ventured to whisper this to Thorgiva.

The monks could think of nothing now but the death of King Edmund; and as they walked, Elswitha told them all she could remember having heard about his capture and death.

It seemed that the king had tried to escape from his enemies, and had hidden himself under a bridge, but the gold spurs on his feet were seen by a bridal party on their way home in the evening, and they informed the Danes where he was hiding.

Redwald in his anger was ready to pronounce a curse upon all weddings, but Osric laid his hand upon his arm. "Nay, nay, my brother, it were well, I ween, if all the world were as we are; but there will ever be some who, despising the future honour and glory, grasp their pleasure in this life; and since God doth not forbid it, let us not curse it."

"Then let evil mischance overtake every wedded pair crossing this bridge on their way home from the wedding!" said Redwald, fiercely; at which Elswitha smiled and said,

"I have heard that even the saint-king himself uttered some such curse, when he knew who had betrayed him."

"It were well then for all the newly wedded to avoid this bridge in all future times," said Thorgiva; "for the world cannot do without weddings, I trow. Though I say nought against monks, only that too many might be an evil thing."

But Osric shook his head. "Nay, nay, the world hath need of those who, having no cares of their own, can help to bear its burden of care and sorrow, and bind up its bleeding wounds: and who have leisure from their own worldly concerns to do this, but the brethren and sisters who have vowed themselves to a life of poverty and chastity, that they may serve God better by serving their suffering fellowmen?"

"Yea; so long as monks can teach and work, and provide a refuge for the helpless better than other men, their work in the world must be the best work," said Thorgiva; "but if ever monks should forget that this is their work, the world were better without them, I trow."

They were nearing Eglesdune by this time, and Osric grew strangely silent as they went on to see the spot where the body of the martyr lay in its unhonoured grave. Elswitha was more anxious now to see the village once more, and ascertain whether any of her old friends still survived.

Of course the special errand upon which they had come had first to be performed, and then, while the monks stood gazing at the bare patch of ground, which Thorgiva had recognized by some mark known only to a few of her kinsfolk, she and Elswitha went to visit some of the people in the village, to ascertain if possible whether she was likely to find any of her own friends among them.

But, alas for her hopes, the Danes held this now, as they held Ea, and were lords paramount of the soil, holding a few of the original inhabitants as their slaves, the rest having been murdered or driven away.

Thorgiva tried to comfort the poor girl, but she did not know how dear the hope had grown lately that she should see her friends once more. Now, however, there was nothing before her but a life in the lonely hermitage with Thorgiva and her baby, and she could not help a little shrinking at the prospect.

The monks had decided in their own minds that another church must be built over the remains of the martyr-king; but to do this, and secure it against destruction, it would be necessary not only to enclose it, but to preach the gospel to these Danes of Eglesdune, as they had at Ea.

It was evident they were not strangers; several who had visited Ea recognized them again, and one man gave them a pressing invitation to stay and sing some of the wonderful sagas they had heard of, and this Osric thought was too favourable an opportunity to be lost.

A meeting in the mead-hall was hastily convened, and here both the monks sang the famous hymns of Cædmon in turn, and then spoke to the people, declaring that God had sent to them the message of pardon for all their sins, if they would accept Jesus as their God and Saviour.

This they could not promise to do at once; but they had heard that their neighbours of Ea had forsaken the worship of Thor, and allowed the sacred fire on his altar to be extinguished; which of course could only mean that they were about to embrace Christianity; and certainly what the Danes of Ea did, they might do; and so they would consider the monks' proposal to build a timber church over the grave of the martyr-king Edmund.

Meanwhile Thorgiva and Elswitha had returned homewards; but, at the sight of the little hut, the disappointment she had felt at finding her native place wholly in the possession of her country's enemies came upon the poor girl afresh, and she could not restrain her tears.

"I had always hoped that God would give me some friends again!" she sobbed.

Thorgiva hardly knew what to say to comfort her, for she felt that it was she who had made this poor girl's life so desolate; and what could she do now to repair the cruel wrong which in the days of her darkness and paganism she had committed? It came upon her all at once that she ought to do something, that the God whom she had vowed in her heart to serve would expect this service at her hand; and, after all, it was not so difficult, for she had grown to love Elswitha lately, and had felt secretly glad that she had no friends at Eglesdune to whom she could go, for Thorgiva would miss her very much.

But what could she do? What ought she to do? Elswitha had always done everything for her and baby, and declared that she liked doing it, when Thorgiva had said she would do some of this necessary work for herself. She noticed now that the girl shivered as she looked up at the budding trees, and then at the little hut; and she said, hastily, "Dost thou dread the solitude, Elswitha?"

"Yes, I am growing weary of it; but I must bear it." And then the tears burst forth afresh.

Thorgiva did not reply, but Elswitha's words

had evidently set her thinking, and shortly after they had reached home, and had had something to eat, she said she would like to pay a visit to her brother, if Elswitha would mind the baby.

The girl looked surprised. "Going to the village!" she said; "would it not be well to wait until father Osric comes back from Eglesdune?"

But Thorgiva shook her head. She had a strong suspicion that her errand might not altogether please the monk, and so she wanted to do it at once. "My friends are willing to forgive me for being a Christian, and Lodbrog my brother sent a kindly message by father Osric," she said.

"But didst thou not say, when he told thee of this, that thou wouldst never go back to the village again, even to see thy friends?" said Elswitha.

Her companion did not wait to hear more. "I have altered my mind, Elswitha," she said shortly; and the next minute she was gone, leaving the baby in Elswitha's lap.

But, once out in the wood, Thorgiva did not seem in such a hurry to reach the village. What Elswitha had said was true; she had declared she would never again see the faces of those who had slain her husband, and what it cost her now to overcome the repugnance she felt at seeing and being seen, no one knew but herself. It was a hard battle she had to fight, and her pride would not let her yield easily; for she knew that in going back to the village she would be going to meet insult

and ridicule, and many obstacles would be put
in the way of her serving the God of their Angle
slaves. She would not be able to go to the feasts
and merry-makings, and friends would take this
as a slight, and the way she now desired her child
should be educated would be an offense to every
Dane in the village. This last consideration almost
made her turn back, and resign herself to a life of
solitude with Elswitha in the forest, but that the
remembrance of Elswitha again urged her to go
forward. Difficult as it would be for her to live as a
Christian in the midst of her heathen relatives, she
would and must do it—she would and must strive
to do something to atone for the cruel wrong that
had desolated that poor girl's life.

Chapter XV

Œlswitha

IT was dusk when Thorgiva reached the village; and she was not sorry, for the friendly shadows of evening would screen her from the curious gaze of many, and it was this she shrunk from more than anything else, the half-wondering, half-pitying glances of her former neighbours.

When once the village was reached, she walked as quickly as she could, neither pausing nor looking aside until she got to her brother's house, and her hand lay on the heavy wooden latch-pin. There was no need to ask if he was at home, for through the eye-hole near the door she could hear his voice calling loudly to some of his slaves, and so, without wasting time to knock, she opened the door and went in.

Lodbrog stared as his sister entered, but he was too glad to see her once more to express much surprise, for the monk had told him that she utterly rejected his offer of restoring her house and land.

"Thorgiva!" "Lodbrog!" was all that either could utter; for the recollection of the past almost overcame them, now that they stood face to face once more.

"Lodbrog, I am a Christian, and I want to serve and please the God of the Christians; I forgive thee," she said, in a low voice.

But Lodbrog only stared. He had not asked for her forgiveness, would not own even to himself that he needed it for anything he had done, but he would not tell Thorgiva this just now. He loved his sister, and was glad she had come, and he said so, ignoring her words, or thinking of them only as an evidence that this Christianity must weaken the character, or Thorgiva would have come not with forgiveness, but revenge.

"The monk told me thou didst desire to spend thy life apart from all thy kind. Did he lie?" asked the Dane.

"Nay, nay: I told father Osric but yesterday that I would never come hither again, but thou seest I have come."

"And right glad am I to see thee, Thorgiva! Thou wilt take the land now for thy child, I trow," said her brother.

"Yes; the house and the land that was Thordstein's shall be his child's, and I will abide in it until he be grown."

"Now thou speakest like a wise woman, like my sister Thorgiva; and all the neighbours will rejoice when they hear thou art coming to thine old home again."

But Thorgiva could only shudder now at the thought of coming back once more to the scene of her husband's death, and she hastened to change the subject.

"I shall not dwell alone with the child. Dost thou remember my Angle slave, Elswitha?"

"She whom thou didst devote to Odin?"

Thorgiva nodded. It seemed that each and every subject referred to must revive some old wrong committed, or some deed of blood she would fain forget.

"The girl did escape, then: that false priest assured us that she could not get away; that the magic he had used would bring her back to the sacred grove, and that she came that night and he completed the sacrifice."

"It was false. The monks found her as they journeyed hither. She was trying to find her way to Eglesdune, but fell and injured her foot, and was lame for a long time."

"Thou hast told the secret of Eglesdune, Thorgiva?" said her brother, a little anxiously.

"I have been there with the monks, and Elswitha too, and—" but there Thorgiva stopped. How could her brother understand the newborn thoughts and hopes and desires of her heart? She had better keep secret at present her motive for wishing to return to the village; so she only said,

"Elswitha will come with me, to help me with the child."

"Thou hast claimed her for thy slave again?" said Lodbrog, questioningly.

Thorgiva started at the question; for such an idea as "claiming" Elswitha had never crossed her mind; but it showed her that she must be cautious how she spoke to the poor girl, lest she should think this too.

"Nay, nay," she hastened to reply; "I gave her to Odin, and as she hath escaped from him she is free."

Lodbrog laughed. "Will she come with thee?" he asked the next minute.

"I shall be sorely grieved if she should not; but I do not think she will like to be separated from my little Æthelstan."

"Æthelstan! That is thy child—named after our king, I trow."

"Yes, and—"

"Thorgiva! thou wilt bring up the child as a Dane," interrupted her brother.

"Yes; as a Dane and a Christian: but he shall not be taught to glory in being the son of a Viking—a sea-thief, as you and I and all our children are. I will teach him—"

"Teach him what thou wilt, only let him be brave and patient; let him not grow up a weakling," said Lodbrog.

"Thou shalt help me teach him some lessons, an

thou wilt. But now about the house. Thou wilt let thy house-carles clean it? and I should like it made ready for us ere long; make it as much like the Angles' houses we found here"—which Lodbrog understood to mean, "hang the walls with wall-riff or arras, and let there be a few of the Saxon conveniences of life."

Not that Thorgiva herself cared for these things; but in her newly awakened care for Elswitha's comfort she wanted the poor girl to feel, if possible, that it was to be her home, and she was no longer among enemies, but friends.

She would not linger long with her brother, for she was anxious to get back to her hut in the forest before it was quite dark, lest she should lose her way. Elswitha too would be anxious if she was absent much longer, and her baby would be crying.

So Thorgiva hurried back with even more speed than she came, and succeeded in eluding all the gossips and most of the prying eyes of the neighbourhood.

When she was seated with her baby on her lap once more, and Elswitha was on the floor at her feet, where she so often sat now, she drew the girl's head down upon her knee, with a motherly caressing movement, as she whispered, "Elswitha, I am very sorry; I wish I could undo the past. I wish God could let us undo all the evil of our past lives as well as repent of it;" and Thorgiva sighed as she spoke.

"Nay! we cannot undo the evil; but I think sometimes that God doth make the evil work for good," said Elswitha.

"It may be as thou sayest; but the evil is a sore trouble, and I would that I could atone for all, since I cannot undo it."

Something in her tone caused Elswitha to look up; and she said, "What dost thou wish to do?"

"To make thee happier—to give thee friends," said Thorgiva, quietly.

But Elswitha only shook her head. "My Father in heaven doth give me sweet peace and content sometimes. Friends I may not have again, for they are all in heaven, I trow."

"Nay, nay, Elswitha, not all," said Thorgiva, in a pained voice; "thou dost not count me for thine enemy now?" she whispered.

"Nay! not mine enemy, but—" and Elswitha stopped.

"But thou wilt not have me for thy friend?" said Thorgiva, quickly.

"Nay, nay, I said not so, I—I knew not that thou wouldst be my friend; for thou art Thorgiva the Dane, and I am but thine Angle slave."

"Nay, nay, thou art a free woman—as free as any Dane," said Thorgiva, "and I ask thee now to let me be thy friend—thy mother, an thou wilt let me. It would be hard to part with thee now, Elswitha, and my little babe would miss thee too."

"But why shouldst thou talk of parting? Art thou going away?" asked the girl.

"Only to the village—to live among the Dane-folk again."

Elswitha started. "Oh, what shall I do without thee?" she said.

"Thou wilt come with us—come and be my daughter; I am almost old enough to be thy mother," said Thorgiva.

"But the Dane-folk!" said the girl; "what will they say to the slave Elswitha, who was devoted to Odin?"

"My brother hath heard of thy escape, and doth rejoice at it, and many others will do likewise. Thou hast heard that the sacred fire on the altar of Thor hath not been burning for many weeks now."

Elswitha nodded. "What can that mean?" she said.

"That the Danes are about to become Christians; not by charter with King Alfred only, but of our own free choice—the choice of a free people," she added.

But to Elswitha the news seemed too wonderful to be true. These fierce Danes, Christians!— somehow it did not give her joy to hear it; she could not rejoice just yet that they should be made partakers of the same heavenly blessings as her own nation, who having lost all earthly hope and joy and comfort, had only the future world to

WONDERFUL: *strange, amazing*

look forward to as a recompense for the trials and sorrows of this.

But now, if their enemies had not only the kingdom of East Anglia, of which her people had been robbed, but were made sharers in their glorious hope of the future, what had they as a recompense for all their toil and suffering here? She had forgiven Thorgiva, and was willing that she should share with her the joys of heaven; but that this should be for all Danes—Elswitha could only shake her head in sadness. She was a long way from being a perfect saint, and happily she knew it.

But her ruminations were interrupted by Thorgiva telling her what her errand to her brother had been about. "Lodbrog hath determined to abide at Ea when the freemen assemble for the Al-thing at Thetford this year. There will be no campaign—little to talk of but the number of white shields among us, which will cause much grumbling among those whose valour hath not been proven. Lodbrog hath no white shield to mourn over, for he is a warrior tried and proved, though he be many years younger than I; so he saith it is meet for him to abide at home, and dig and sow his field, as the monks would fain persuade all our Dane-folk to do."

It is not surprising that Elswitha could not rejoice at this piece of news, as Osric had done; for she had looked forward to the departure of the Danes: they might go to Mercia, or Wessex, or sail for their own savage North; she cared not which,

RUMINATIONS: *thoughts*

so that they left East Anglia, and her friends and kinsmen could return and take possession of their own again.

Poor girl! she forgot that the Angles were but a few feeble folk like herself, and that if this colony of Danes departed, they would be succeeded by another as savage as these were when led by the cruel Ubba, the murderer of King Edmund. The present usurpers had grown somewhat civilized by contact with the Angles, and submitting to the laws of King Alfred, and were more than half-ashamed of the royal martyr's death now, to say nothing of the work of the monks among them. Therefore, for these to leave Ea now would be a calamity rather than a blessing to the few remaining Angles.

Thorgiva noticed her silence, but did not know the cause; and she went on to explain how she had desired her brother to make her house as home-like as possible; and how she intended to sow her field, and make a garden, with fruit-trees and flowers in it, near the house; which would be quite a novelty in Ea, for the old gardens had all been trampled down, and the fruit-trees torn up long since.

Now that she had made up her mind to go back, Thorgiva was impatient to make the removal as soon as possible, and Elswitha, who could not bear the thought of being separated from the child, was willing to go at once; and so, early the next morning, Thorgiva paid another visit to Lodbrog, to ask him to have the house prepared that very day, as she and Elswitha, with the baby, were coming the day following.

"It is like thee, Thorgiva," laughed her brother; "but the house shall be ready for thee and thy Angle friend."

"Yes; she is my friend," said Thorgiva, "and I would have thee tell all the Dane-folk this before we come."

Lodbrog bowed. "I will do thy bidding," he said; and he took good care to let it be known among the gossips that although Thorgiva was a Christian, she had a will of her own, like every other Danish woman, and it would be well for them to remember this before they attempted to interfere with anything they might not quite approve of.

So when Osric and Redwald returned from Eglesdune, where they were detained three days, they found to their consternation that the little hermitage was tenantless, and everything belonging to Thorgiva had been removed.

What could it mean? Where could they have gone? Surely someone, some unknown enemy—the priest of Thor perhaps, had come and carried them off!

If it was so, they had certainly been added to the "noble army of martyrs" long ere this; and the monks betook themselves to the abbey, thinking of the loss they had suffered in the removal of their saint Elswitha.

CONSTERNATION: *sudden alarm or dismay*

No suspicion of the real state of affairs ever crossed the mind of either, for although Osric had thought it just possible that Thorgiva would return to the village on her brother's invitation, she had assured him she would not, that she never wished to leave the forest and Elswitha again.

Elswitha certainly would not go to live with the "filthy pagan crew" again of her own free will, and so the two sorrow-stricken brethren went home mourning; and it was not until Redwald went out with his fishing-lines to catch something for their evening meal, that he heard from some of the Dane-folk of the removal of Thorgiva to her old home.

"And Elswitha?—didst thou not hear of her, my brother?" asked Osric, quickly.

"Yes; she hath gone back to the Danelagh with Thorgiva," replied the young monk.

"Then Thorgiva hath enforced her to this, and I must tell her that she is no longer her slave." And Osric left the preparation of the meal, though they were both very hungry, and went at once to the village to restore Elswitha to liberty and the solitude of the hermitage. But he heard, to his grief and surprise, that Elswitha had returned of her own free will, and that she had no wish to go back to her saintly life of contemplation.

"I can think of God my Father here as I did before, and I can talk to little Æthelstan about His love; and by and by he will begin to understand

DANELAGH: *the area of England controlled by the Danes; literally "Dane-law"* what I mean when I tell him he has a Father in heaven, Who loves him as deeply and tenderly as his mother can," said Elswitha, when Osric would have persuaded her that the earthly cares of a life with Thorgiva in the Danelagh here would certainly draw her soul away from God.

"This babe hath an immortal soul too: and he will need to be taught how a Christian should live, and—"

"Nay: but what of his mother? Is not she a Christian?" said Osric, quickly.

"Yes: as she saith sometimes, she is learning to be a Christian, but she hath much to unlearn too, for she hath been a pagan all her life, and cannot quite cast off many things she hath no wish her child should learn."

It was useless to argue the point any further. Osric saw that, and wisely gave it up; but it was a bitter disappointment to him to find that she loved this little child so much that she could not give him up for a life of rapt contemplation, to which he certainly thought God had called her.

He went home slowly and sadly, resolving to see her again shortly, and if she still declined to be convinced that she was forsaking a high vocation for the sake of teaching this child, he would then hasten his departure to Thetford, and ask the advice of the brethren there.

Chapter XVI

Eastertide

BEFORE the Danes set out for Thetford, their great festival in honour of Astargydia or Easter, the goddess of love, was to be celebrated; and soon after the return of Thorgiva to the village the whole community was busy preparing for the feast. Thus far the sacred grove and altar of Thor had not been approached by anyone, for, however much they might doubt the power of their old gods, no one would have ventured to interfere with what had been set apart to his service; and so, when it was discovered one morning that the sacred fire was once more burning on the altar, kindled by no visible hands, the sensation that it caused may well be imagined.

Who could have lighted it? asked one and another, as they stood gazing at the wreaths of smoke curling up to the sky. But only solemn headshakes came in response to the question, though doubtless it was in readiness for the coming festival that it had been lighted, and it might be taken as an invitation to commemorate it in the usual fashion, instead of going to the new church, as the monks had been persuading them to do.

Osric had talked to them several times lately about this feast of Astargydia; for the myth that underlay the rough ceremonial of these Danes was the yearly resurrection of Nature, when the sun returned from its wintry sleep of death to clothe the earth with verdure and fill men's hearts with joy and gladness. Now Osric had tried to lift the thoughts of the Danes a step higher than this, and show them the Resurrection of the Gospel, the Resurrection of Christ, and what St. Paul had taught concerning it—that they were to put away the old works of darkness in which they had lived and delighted so long, and rise to newness of life, which meant learning to become Christians, not merely by charter with King Alfred, but in kindness and temperance, honesty and peace.

Not very palatable doctrines these to such people as the Danes; but Osric had been long enough in the neighbourhood now to convince them that he was their friend, and so they had listened and given a half-promise to come to the church on Easter day, and lay aside the old heathen rites for this once.

But the sight of the sacred fire burning once more altered all this, for towards evening the priest of Thor and Odin once more appeared among them, and asked with well-feigned astonishment

VERDURE: *lush greenery*
TEMPERANCE: *self-control*
PALATABLE: *acceptable*

who had kept the sacred fire burning during his absence, but was too crafty to wait for an answer, busying himself in the usual way in readiness for the coming festival, quite as a matter of course, and as though nothing had happened to interrupt his connection with the people in his sacred office.

It would be hard to say what the people themselves thought of the matter: to many, perhaps most of them, the eating, drinking, and revelry that followed was the only significant fact of the whole ceremony, and so long as this continued they cared little for sacred fires or prayers in the church; one or the other was a question of indifference to them now, for they cared little for any god.

Lodbrog tried to arouse them to repudiate the priest, who had carried a spear in defiance of the rules of his order, but they only laughed in a good-tempered, indifferent fashion, and told him to let the gods fight out the quarrel by themselves or their messengers, the priest and monks.

To Osric it was a bitter disappointment when he heard of the return of the priest of Thor, and saw the smoke curling up among the budding trees of the sacred grove. He had hoped to see the church full this Eastertide, and he and Redwald had planned how they might forward some harmless merry-making, that should take the place of the usual wild orgies and reconcile the Danes to the change. They had not asked, they did not expect them to give up their old feast entirely; but the

REPUDIATE: *reject the authority of*
ORGIES: *unrestrained rituals*

festival might be celebrated in a Christian manner, and be made the means of recommending
Christianity to them. And so the disappointment
was bitter indeed to the monks, when they saw the
preparations that were going forward.

It was a time of anxiety to Thorgiva too, for she
had grown very hopeful concerning her brother
Lodbrog lately; but whether he would be able to
withstand the temptations this feast of Astargydia offered, it would be hard to say, for it was not
merely the eating and drinking that went forward,
but the meeting with friends and relatives who had
settled in neighbouring villages and rarely visited
their kinsfolk except on the occasion of a sacred
festival.

She went with her trouble to Osric at last, plainly
confessing that it would be a trial to her to abstain
from all the village merry-making.

"Then, my daughter, we will have a church
festival, and I will sing the songs of Cædmon to
all who will come and listen," said Osric, prompt-
ly; and he and Redwald set to work at once to
gather green boughs and such hardy wild flowers as the forest afforded to decorate the unfinished little church, while Thorgiva went back to
the village, and announced that Christians too
kept the feast of Easter, as well as pagans, and
that the monks would sing their wonderful sagas
to all who liked to go to the church and listen to
them.

She and Elswitha, Lodbrog, and one or two others entered most warmly into the monks' plan of providing a counter attraction to the heathen feast; and this no doubt was the origin of church-ales and other scandals abolished by the Reformation. In the field adjoining the abbey, fires were lighted and a boar roasted, in emulation of the oxen sacrificed in the sacred grove, and afterwards eaten by the worshipers. There was no lack of good ale either at the church feast, for the thane, anxious to please his people, sent a goodly quantity to the abbey as well as to the sacred grove.

The monks were gratified by this kindness, for it gave them some prestige in the eyes of the people, and they could not foresee the mischief this compliance with heathen customs would cause. At present it did little harm, and much good, for at this feast the people received their first practical lesson in temperance both in eating and drinking, a new thing to them.

Osric took care to be with them all the time the feast lasted, and both by precept and example inculcated the Christian duty of sobriety: but it needed all his watchful care to keep even Lodbrog within the bounds of decency.

Thorgiva, with her baby and Elswitha, brought her kinsfolk, who had come to see her, to the church to hear the songs of Cædmon; and many others, attracted by the novelty, came also and preferred the more quiet festival here to the noisy

CHURCH-ALES: *church feasts*
INCULCATED: *taught with frequent repetition*
SOBRIETY: *refraining from drunkenness*

reveling going on in the sacred grove: but still, Osric could not forget that after all he had made but one real convert; and although these people were ready enough to join in a church festival, not one had been willing to help him finish building the church and abbey; and so, in spite of the seeming success of this venture, he felt sadly depressed before it came to an end.

Meanwhile the priest of Thor conceived himself grossly insulted by these monks daring to hold a festival while he was officiating at the sacred grove of the gods. At first he had laughed at the monks' plans; but when he found that many went to listen to their songs, he began to fear that he should lose his power over the people if this was allowed to continue, and so he denounced, and even forbade the worshipers of Thor to approach the abbey lands. This was an unwise step to take with such proud, independent people as the Danes, and a few got up at once and walked off, to see what the monks were doing; others, less daring, but no less curious, took care to go the next day and take a part in the Christian festival; and the priest, finding that words and warnings were alike unheeded, at length decided to go himself and drive the monks away.

It was the last day of the feast, and just as the evening shadows were stealing over the forest, that he took this desperate resolution. All day he had watched with growing rage the decreased

CONCEIVED: *imagined*

numbers who came to the sacrifice, and it needed but a word of grumbling about there being no human victims this time, to send him boiling with wrath to the church, where the people were now assembled for the vesper service.

The little uncouth building, that was scarcely larger than a barn, was nearly full of worshipers, or rather listeners; for the evening service had concluded, and Osric was singing one of the songs of Cædmon, when suddenly in stalked the tall, white-robed priest of Thor. Pausing on the threshold, he looked round upon the people, like a schoolmaster who has discovered a party of truants, and speaking in a loud tone he said, "Ye Danes are bewitched; leave this accursed place, and let me smite this monk as he stands!"

A low growl was heard from one or two of those standing near, but no one attempted to leave the building. This enraged the priest still more, and lifting his arm threateningly, he thundered, "Leave this church, before I pronounce its doom! Will ye Danes, Vikings' sons, come cringing to a weak beggarly God, Who was scourged like any Angle slave?"

"Blaspheme not the name of the Highest, false priest!" said Osric, now stepping forward to bar his approach to the altar.

"Who art thou, slave, that darest to speak to the priest of Thor?" And, as he spoke, he attempted to push his way past the monk. But the monk was as

UNCOUTH: *crudely built*
BLASPHEME: *insult or speak against God*

tall and powerfully built as the priest of Thor; and resolutely maintained his ground.

Nothing would have pleased the Danes better than to see these two engaged in a hand-to-hand fight; and they shouted and yelled, first to the priest, and then to the monk, urging them on to the fray. Little did they care which was worsted, or what the cause of the quarrel might be; it was enough for them that a fight was in prospect, and the fact that it was between the messengers of rival gods only gave zest to the fun.

But Osric was resolved that his little church should not be desecrated by such a scene as a fight would cause, although he was equally determined not to allow the altar to be approached by this pagan priest. So he stood as firm as a rock, and calmly told the priest he should not approach any closer.

The priest was almost mad with rage now, and cursed Osric by every god in his calendar—curses so loud and deep that some of the more timid shivered as they heard them, and eagerly watched to see if the monk did fall dead at his enemy's feet.

This war of words, however, did not suit everybody; it was time something more effectual was done, and so one cried out, "If Thor won't hear, and do thy bidding, knock the monk down thyself."

But this was not so easy of an accomplishment. It was evident that Osric knew something about fighting, for he had put himself in an attitude of

defense, so that his antagonist, wild with rage as
he was, hesitated to strike the first blow, but tried
hard to push his way past his adversary.

"Strike him fair in front!" shouted one of the
half-tipsy giants who had followed the priest.

"He is waiting for the gods to do his bidding,
since we have refused," said another, mockingly.

At this moment the priest made a desperate
lunge at Osric, and succeeded in passing him:
there was the gleam of a knife as he raised his arm,
and with a groan the monk staggered forward and
fell on his face.

"The gods have smitten him!" cried the priest,
triumphantly. But the next moment he was seized
by two or three of the angry Danes; and before
he could conceal it, one of the sacred knives was
snatched from his hand.

The whole church was in an uproar now, everybody vowing vengeance against the priest of Thor;
some, because he had degraded his sacred office,
and others, who thought little of this, protesting
against the cowardice of striking a man in the
back: for these Danes, amid all their vices, were
notable lovers of fair play, and so it was small mercy their priest would get now.

But as Redwald and Lodbrog were raising Osric, he saw that his church was likely to be defiled
by the murder of the priest of Thor on the very
steps of the altar, and he implored Redwald to
leave him and save the priest.

HALF-TIPSY: *half-drunk*

"But thou art wounded, my brother," said his companion, in a voice of agony.

Much against his will, Lodbrog turned to the combatants close by: "Cease this fighting," he said, in a commanding tone; and for once his countrymen were willing to obey, although they would not relinquish their prisoner.

"He is a false coward, and no priest!" they cried.

"Drive him away then, and put out his sacred fire," said Lodbrog, seizing this as a favourable moment for carrying out a plan he had begun to form in his own mind.

This hint was enough, for the angry crowd instantly rushed from the church and down to the sacred grove, bent on the destruction of all they could lay hands upon. The sacred fire was swept from the altar, and the altar itself partially beaten down. Then they hacked at the sacred trees, and scattered the various implements of sacrifice, and worked as much mischief as they could all round.

It was a wild outbreak of fury, uncontrolled by reason or consideration of any kind. The old faith had long ceased to have any firm hold upon their minds, and its priest had offended them; and so he and the outward symbols of his religion were alike swept away; for while one party were desecrating the sacred grove, another had driven the priest of Thor out of Ea, threatening to slaughter him if ever he returned.

Meanwhile Osric had been carried to his cell, and his wound examined. It was not so severe as

was at first feared, and the leechcraft of Redwald,
and his own knowledge of what was necessary in
such cases, with a few days' entire rest, almost restored him; so that by the time the Danes began to
gather for their annual journey to Thetford, Osric was so far restored that he decided to go with
them.

Chapter XVII

At Thetford

WITH the first contingent of freemen which left Ea to attend the Al-thing, or general council, Osric journeyed to Thetford, to see how it fared with his brethren there, and to discuss with father Dunstan the case of Elswitha: for she positively declined to leave Thorgiva, and another fear was creeping into his heart on her account.

He found the brethren at Thetford had had fewer trials and greater encouragements to tell of than himself; for the king, remembering his promise to King Alfred, had openly professed the Christian religion, and most of his officers had done the same.

This example set by their rulers had been followed by many of the people, although some among them grumbled at the change. But as the king did not attempt to force this new religion upon them, but left it to their own free choice, they could not say much, although the priests tried hard to incite them to rebellion. But the numbers at the old pagan temple grew less and less, while the church, from which the golden idols had been carried, was crowded with worshipers, and a second one had been built, and an abbey also: for if this wise Saxon Alfred—the wisest and bravest and richest king they had ever heard of—if *he* received his wisdom and riches from this God of the Christians, surely it would be folly for them to refuse such good gifts; especially when He had sent special messengers to them, offering to be their God. Of course, as the God of Angle-land, He expected them to worship Him: Odin came to the North, and was the god of Northmen, but now they had left Daneland, and crossed the sea, Odin must be left behind—this was not his kingdom, and it would be useless for them to enter into the quarrels of the gods. Let Odin fight his own battle with this God of the Christians, and if he could drive Him from His place as the God of Angle-land, well—they would follow Odin; but meanwhile, it was their best policy to worship this great, strong, wise God, who had helped King Alfred to regain his kingdom of Wessex.

This was the reasoning that actuated many, nay most, of those who worshiped in the church of Thetford; but Osric did not know this, and, thinking of his solitary convert in Ea, and of all the difficulties and discouragements that beset them there, he could not help feeling that perhaps after all they had made a mistake in leaving Thetford.

ACTUATED: *motivated*

The two brethren who had left him last autumn were here still: they had found plenty to do in building and furnishing the church and abbey, and draining the outlying lands given them by the king.

Now that Osric had arrived, however, they were to carry the news of their success to their own monastery in Mercia; and if Egbert or any of the other brethren desired to return with them, Osric prayed the prior to send them. He also sent tidings of the discovery of the martyr-king's grave at Eglesdune; and if brethren could be spared, a church might and ought to be built there.

Having dispatched the messengers, he would fain have returned to Ea, but Dunstan pressed him to remain until the council came to an end; for his presence would doubtless be a restraint upon the warlike restlessness of the meeting. In this, however, they had not taken into account the numbers who would come straight from the altars of Thor with white shields for the second or third time to attend the yearly Al-thing. The men of Thetford and Ea were disposed to turn their attention to the cultivation of their lands and the building of better houses, now that the monks had come among them and taught them the advantage of these things; but those who had lived at a distance from these places, and knew nothing of what was passing there, came up eager as ever to enter upon some campaign against their neighbours, and determined not to return home with white shields again.

To restrain the more eager of these was utterly impossible. The utmost King Guthrum could do was to keep them from marching at once to Mercia; and it was only the news that some Danes were going in their long boats to France, and would accept the service of any Vikings who would go with them, that saved that kingdom from being ravaged again.

So the Al-thing broke up hastily, hundreds of the freemen marching straight to their boats, eager now for the conquest of France and the fighting and spoil that would fall to their share.

A few of the younger and more restless of the Dane-folk went too; but many went south to their homes again, resolving to drain and cultivate their lands, as the people of Thetford were doing. Osric returned with these; for he had arranged that if Egbert or other brethren came this year, they should journey by way of Broderickworth, through the country of the South-folk: for the Danes in that part of the country were anxious to share in the blessing that had come to Thetford and Ea, and readily promised to help the monks forward in their journey.

But, in spite of all the encouraging signs of their mission being a success, Osric returned to Ea feeling sadly depressed and troubled. He thought of the unfinished church and abbey, of the very little anxiety felt by the people to get the church completed, although the priest of Thor had been banished; and last, but not least, Elswitha's unwillingness to enter upon a monastic life. He had consulted with father Dunstan about this, but the elder monk could not advise him in the matter. He could only deplore that the intense love for a secluded life seemed gradually to have died out, so that it was difficult now to obtain brethren and sisters for the monasteries and convents that had escaped the ravaging hands of the Danes.

Perhaps it was because so many had fallen helpless victims into the hands of these fierce conquerors, and men thought of saving themselves from a like fate, that so few cared to enter a monastery now. Dunstan could only conjecture that this might be the cause: he knew not what to say about Elswitha.

Meanwhile the girl had decided the question of her own future in a way that almost overwhelmed her good friend the monk. Osric had no sooner returned than Thorgiva came to renew her request for baptism, saying that Lodbrog, her brother, desired to be baptized at the same time.

Osric looked surprised. "Lodbrog thy brother doth desire baptism," he said, "but—but who hath taught him to seek this?"

"He hath grown very fond of my little Æthelstan, and hath heard Elswitha talking to the child in her wondrous wise, simple fashion, which he said he could understand better even than the wonderful sagas thou hast sung."

The monk looked up sharply as she mentioned the name of Elswitha, and said, "Hath she not grown tired of tending the child yet? Doth she say nought of returning to the forest?"

Thorgiva fidgeted about in a manner quite unlike her usual calm, haughty demeanour; but at length she managed to say, "Nay, holy father, I do not think she hath any desire to return to the forest, for—for—" and there she stopped, for she knew that the news she had come to impart would be very distasteful to the monk, although it was just what she had been wishing might happen.

"What wouldst thou say, my daughter?" asked Osric anxiously, half-fearing what the truth might be.

"Lodbrog doth desire Elswitha to become his wife," said Thorgiva.

Osric started. "Then she must leave thee, Thorgiva, and return to the forest."

"But wherefore should she do this?"

"Canst thou ask such a question? Can a Christian maiden like Elswitha wed a—?" Osric had all but uttered the words "a filthy pagan," when he bethought himself, and remembered to whom he was speaking.

But the tone in which Osric had spoken, without these words, was enough to rouse Thorgiva's proud spirit; and she answered haughtily, "Nay!

BETHOUGHT HIMSELF: *considered*

it were an honour for an Angle like Elswitha to marry a Dane like Lodbrog. Such marriages often come to pass," she added.

"But not with such maidens as Elswitha. She hath a higher vocation, and she will—she must—desire a life of calm contemplation, untroubled by earthly cares; especially such cares as will beset her if—" He stopped, for he could not pronounce the word "wife."

"But Elswitha doth not desire this life of contemplation," said Thorgiva.

"Nay! she hath been troubled by the importunities of Lodbrog. I will talk with her of this."

"And about our baptism?" said his visitor; for in the eagerness of his anxiety about Elswitha, Osric had not replied to her first question upon this matter.

"Thou and thy brother desire to profess thy belief in the Lord Christ our Saviour?" said Osric, musingly; "I will talk of this to thee again, but I must see Elswitha without delay."

Thorgiva knew that Osric would use all his influence to induce the girl to forsake her brother and embrace a monastic life; and it greatly troubled her, for hers was no mere profession of Christianity. She had learned to love the Lord Jesus Christ, and was most anxious that her family should do the same; and for her brother to take a Christian wife, and such a wife as she knew Elswitha would be, was one of the things she now most heartily desired.

IMPORTUNITIES: *persistent requests*

That Lodbrog really loved Elswitha there could be no doubt; and Thorgiva remembered that if she had listened to her brother her parents would not have been devoted to Odin; all which she told her, while Elswitha could recall many little acts of kindness stealthily performed for her by the young Dane, when she was a downtrodden slave in his sister's household.

But the two women had little time to talk after Thorgiva's return from the abbey; for Osric followed her almost immediately, so anxious was he to save Elswitha from her present danger, as he chose to consider it.

But Elswitha did not see the danger: "I can serve God here in the village, as the wife of Lodbrog," said Elswitha, timidly.

"But, my daughter, hast thou considered the holy vocation thou art forsaking—the life of heavenly meditation and prayer?"

"But—but, holy father, thou didst tell me once that God sent men into the world to work as well as pray. There is no work for me to do in the forest; while here—"

"No work for thee in the forest!" repeated Osric; "nay, thou art called to the highest work—to pray for these evil Dane-folk, and—"

"But I would rather stay here with them, where I can work and pray too," said Elswitha, "than stay in the forest, where I can do nothing but pray."

"But think of what thy work here will be—the common earthly cares that any woman can perform. Hast thou thought of this, Elswitha?"

The girl hung down her head, and a faint colour stole into her cheek as she answered, "Lodbrog saith no other woman can do the work for him that I can."

At this moment Thorgiva came in, and eagerly rejoined, "It is true, holy father; for if Elswitha had not been here to hold him back, Lodbrog would have gone to France with the other Vikings, when the news came from the Al-thing that there was a campaign at last. Our Danes, when they would win the favour of a woman, must prove themselves worthy Vikings and warriors by doing battle with any or all who come in their way; but Lodbrog knew this was not the way to win Elswitha, and so he is learning the ways of peaceful men, sowing his fields and preparing his house, as few of the Dane-folk do."

Of course it was for this, that they might learn the arts of civilization as well as the religion of peace, that Osric had come among these people, and he could not but feel pleased that such a ruling spirit as Lodbrog was among his kinsfolk should so eagerly take to the habits of a settled people; but the price to be paid for this, the sacrifice of Elswitha—for he looked upon it as a sacrifice—was too much, and he could not reconcile his mind to it.

Thorgiva and Elswitha both agreed that it would be better not to tell Lodbrog of the opposition of Osric to their marriage; for it might be that he would attribute unworthy motives to the monk, which would greatly hinder the work he had at heart. They both hoped and believed that when he found Elswitha was firm in her resolution he would cease to oppose it.

Meanwhile Osric was revolving a plan in his mind, by means of which he thought he could interpose an effectual barrier to this hateful marriage. Elswitha would never consent to marry any but a Christian. Lodbrog was not yet baptized. Now, if Osric could profess himself dissatisfied with him on some point of Christian faith, this might be refused, or at least postponed, and meanwhile Elswitha might be persuaded to return to the forest.

But even while he was ruminating upon the plan, his cheek flushed, and he unconsciously quickened his pace, as though the tempter was following him, and could be outdistanced. And truly the temptation did follow him, now the evil suggestion was once admitted. At meals, or work, at prayers in the church, or in consultation with Redwald, the whisper seemed to come, "Refuse the Dane baptism, and Elswitha must go to the forest; she cannot marry a pagan."

Osric grew restless and unhappy: the only relief he could find from the mental torture that

REVOLVING: *turning over*
INTERPOSE: *put between*

now consumed him was in work, and he laboured almost incessantly, either in the fields or in the work of finishing the church, leaving Redwald to sing the sagas of Cædmon, and preach and teach among the Dane-folk.

He dared not trust himself to go into the village now; but often, when Redwald was asleep, he was on his knees before God, battling with the temptation that so sorely beset him, and praying for grace to overcome it. But for a long while the tempter would not be driven away, or if driven away for a short time, returned again, armed with arguments so specious that Osric must fain listen to them, and for the moment yield, and resolve to act upon that view, so favourable to his own wishes.

But though only a man, subject to temptations like other men, Osric was an honest man—honest even with himself; and no sooner had the lie nestled down in his heart than it was routed out again, and the thing stood before him once more, shorn of all its deception, and he almost hated himself for having once encouraged such a thought.

The conflict grew so severe at last that his health began to suffer through it, when there came a timely diversion, a fresh anxiety and care. An Angle slave arrived at the abbey one day with a message to say that a party of monks had lately arrived at Broderickworth, and one brother, Egbert, was ill, and desired brother Osric to go to him with all speed. The walk of twenty miles, with the anxiety

SPECIOUS: *deceptively pleasing*

lest his beloved Egbert should die before he reached the end of his journey, put an end to his thoughts about Elswitha—at least for the present. Egbert was ill and needed him—needed medicine and food, perhaps—that was enough to crowd out even the engrossing thought of Elswitha, and Osric set out at once, anxious to reach the town with as little delay as possible.

Chapter XVIII

The Runaway Brides

THE messenger had by no means exaggerated the pressing need there was for Osric to see Egbert without delay, not merely as his most dear friend, but also as a skillful leech; for in those days the art of healing, like most of the other beneficent arts of life, was in the hands of the monks almost exclusively.

Egbert had not merely been overcome by the fatigue of the journey, but just before he reached Broderickworth he fell from the mule on which he was riding, and broke his leg. His companions carried him into the town, where they were very civilly received by the Danes, who directed them to the monastery of St. Mary, the buildings having escaped the usual destruction directed against monasteries. But the brethren were all dead or driven away, and there was little beyond the bare walls for shelter; still, they were thankful even for this, and sent at once to Osric at Ea, knowing that he would contrive to help them out of their difficulties.

BENEFICENT: *good, kind*

As soon as the usual greetings were over, and Osric had ascertained the condition of his patient, he said, "Egbert cannot journey from hence for many weeks, for he is in great danger, and needeth much care and skillful leechcraft; but we cannot all abide here, and leave our brother alone in Ea; two of ye must journey to Redwald, while I abide here with Egbert and Earpwold, who will be useful to me in nursing our sick brother, and teaching the people in this place." For Osric had no idea of letting the work stand still—this great work of evangelizing the Danes and teaching them some of the arts of a settled people.

Before the brethren departed he charged them with a message to Redwald—that the church should be finished with all speed, and solemnly dedicated to God's service, and then Redwald should baptize Thorgiva and her brother, and afterwards marry Lodbrog to Elswitha.

The brethren looked surprised and somewhat alarmed at having to carry such a message as this to Redwald. "Wilt thou not come thyself to Ea, in time for the chrism-loosing, if thou art not there for the baptism of Thorgiva; and this wedding could take place at the same time?"

But Osric shook his head. "I shall come to Ea as soon as may be, but the church is well-nigh completed now, and it is not meet that the baptisms and this wedding should be delayed much longer." For, having made up his mind now as to the true

ASCERTAINED: *seen for himself*
CHRISM-LOOSING: *a religious ritual involving anointing oil that followed after baptism*

nature of the motives that made him so averse to the marriage of Elswitha, he would no longer give any quarter to the temptation that had so sorely beset him, or even trust himself to see her again, until she had become the wife of Lodbrog.

There were various other matters upon which Redwald had to be advised, and then, when the brethren had departed, it was a relief to turn to Egbert, and hear from him something of what had happened in Mercia during the last year. It was a pleasure to tend and nurse him, soothing to the monk's wounded heart, for, in his bitter self-reproach and condemnation, he had not spared himself, either in outward penances or inward self-abhorrence, when he discovered the weakness of his own heart. To forget himself, and Elswitha, and Lodbrog, and all the concerns of Ea and East Anglia, was an intense relief, and he was ready to enter into any or all the plans Egbert had to propose.

It seemed that on his way hither they had come by rather a circuitous route, that they might halt at the vill of his uncle, his mother's brother; and here he had met with his sister, who had fled from her home to avoid being forced into a disagreeable marriage—a marriage necessary for her father to conclude an advantageous compact with a neighbouring ealdorman many years older than himself, and which was proportionately repulsive to the girl.

ABHORRENCE: *hatred*
CIRCUITOUS: *round about*
COMPACT: *agreement*

"She had thought of the monastic life before she saw me: she had desired to live in the wilderness, like St. Bridget, whom an Irish minstrel had sung about one day when staying at my father's house," said Egbert. "Thyra was so charmed with this minstrelsy that she persuaded the gleeman to teach her the hymn of St. Bridget before he left, and then she would fain teach me, and begged me to help her live like St. Bridget. Hast thou heard her hymn?" he asked.

Osric shook his head. "Wilt thou tell it to me?" he said.

And Egbert, nothing loth, began:—

> "Bridget the victorious she loved not the world;
> She sat on it as the gull sits on the ocean.
> She slept the sleep of a captive mother,
> Mourning after her absent child.
>
> She suffered not much from evil tongues.
> She held the blessed faith of the Trinity;
> Bridget the mother of my Lord of heaven,
> The best among the sons of the Lord.
>
> She was not querulous, nor malevolent,
> She loved not the fierce wrangling of women,
> She was not a backbiting serpent, nor a liar;
> She sold not the Son of God for that which passeth away.
>
> She was not greedy of the goods of this life,
> She gave away without gall, without slackness,
> She was not rough to wayfaring men,
> She handled gently the wretched lepers."

Osric did not think much of the hymn, except as it had roused Egbert's sister to see the hollowness

EALDORMAN: *an Anglo-Saxon official*

of all earthly delights and riches, and inspired her with a desire to live apart from the world, and spend her life in deeds of mercy and charity. But, doubtless, carried about by the wandering Irish minstrel, it would sow the like seeds in many other gentle hearts.

But beyond this Osric thought little of St. Bridget or Thyra either; and he did not pay much attention to the rest of Egbert's story, although he told him of his cousin's description of a party of monks, who had come to the vill one spring day the year before, and how from this description Egbert knew it was his own friends, and had told her he was about to join them.

Egbert's talk about his sister and cousin had sent Osric's thoughts back again to Elswitha; and while Egbert was reciting the hymn of St. Bridget, he was thinking whether it would not be better to give the young monk a word of advice about the danger of a woman's society. He would not spare himself, however humiliating the confession might be, for in making it now it might be the means of saving Egbert from similar pain and difficulty.

So the story was told from beginning to end. But instead of Egbert being shocked and surprised at the grievous sin of which Osric had been guilty, he said, "God made man and woman to dwell together, I trow; and so it is His voice in—"

But Osric hastily put his hands to his ears and turned away. "Hath the devil sent thee to tempt me too?" he exclaimed, bitterly.

"Nay, Osric, I did but tell thee what I believe. Men, such as thou art—monks who have no home-ties, are needful to the world as it is; the world of cruelty and violence, where there is no room for the weak, except in the shelter the Church doth provide. But, Osric, God made not this world to be as it is. The devil hath marred the glorious work of His hands, so that now it is needful to send forth His angels, the monks, to teach men once more that they are men, and not brute beasts; but when the world hath learned this lesson, then the monks' work will be done, I trow, and it were better—"

"Nay, monks are not angels," interrupted Osric, sadly.

"But they are men whom God hath given angels' work to do. It may be that they can do it better than angels could, for men now know that we are men like themselves."

Osric recalled his visit to the mead-hall, and how his hunger had opened a way to their hearts as nothing else could have done; and he wondered whether these sharp-eyed Danes would penetrate his secret concerning Elswitha—a secret he had not known himself until very recently. For in trying to persuade her to return to the forest, his chief desire had been that a sisterhood should be founded there, sisters who might help the women and little children as men, even monks, could not do. He had afterwards to learn that underneath this wish for a sisterhood, to be presided over by Elswitha, there lurked the more personal desire for a continuation of the sweet communion he had often had with her, when the burden of care had been lifted by the bright words of hope and faith and courage she had uttered. She had taught him the blessed hidden meaning of the sweet words, "Our Father;" she had brought God and heaven so near to him that he could not but think of her as a saint. Marriage and Elswitha seemed little short of desecration; and then such a marriage—a wedding of one of God's sweetest, purest angels to "a filthy pagan"! It was not strange that Osric should feel bitterly disappointed.

Egbert, however, took a different view of the matter. He had heard that his eldest cousin was going to be married to a Danish ealdorman, and he thought that these unions with Christian wives would do more to civilize the people than anything monks or nuns could do—an opinion which rather shocked Osric.

So, by way of changing the subject, Egbert begged that the presents he had brought might be unpacked now, for he had not come empty-handed, either from the monastery or his uncle's house.

From the prior he had brought a most valuable gift—a bell for the church. Then there was a covering for the altar, and last, but not the least useful, six horns, scraped and polished until they were almost transparent, and fitted with a socket for a candle. These horn lamps were for the church, for in stormy windy weather the unglazed eyeholes, or windows, made it impossible to use a light.

This was an invention of King Alfred's which the monks were not slow to imitate, as these lanterns would be useful in helping them to keep account of the time more correctly; for in those days the only means of measuring time were candles, made of a precise weight and length, and marked to burn a certain number of hours. Exposed to a draught, they would flare out much quicker than they ought, which disarranged the time-keeping, and was often a source of vexation and annoyance.

Then, besides these lanterns, Egbert had brought some embroidered wall-hangings and silver cups, presents from his uncle, aunt, and cousins, and he begged his friend to choose one of these for himself.

"Nay, nay, but what use have I for a silver cup: and besides, dost thou forget that a monk hath no goods apart from his brethren?" said Osric; and yet, as he finished speaking, he wished he had accepted the gift.

But there was no time to recall his words now, for while they were talking Earpwold came hastily into the room with the news that two Saxon gleemen were at the gate, begging for food and shelter.

"Shelter we can give, but little food have we to spare," concluded Earpwold.

"What we have, we will share with these strangers," said Osric; "bid them enter, Earpwold, and prepare a meal for them if they be hungry."

Earpwold went to do as he was bidden, although he was rather unwilling to give from their scanty store of food, more especially as Egbert was ill, and might need all, and more than all, they could get for him.

The minstrels seemed very glad to get away from the crowd which had followed them through the town to the monastery gate, but they scarcely touched the food that was set before them; indeed, they seemed too much fatigued to eat, and begged Earpwold to let them stay and rest awhile before proceeding on their journey.

So they were shown to the guest-house, or quiet chamber, without delay, taking their harp with them, which was some disappointment to Earpwold, who had resolved to try and play it himself, or ask Osric to take it, and sing one of the songs of Cædmon that he had heard him talk about. Now, however, he would have to wait until the minstrels awoke, when he determined to ask them to play and sing, which they could scarcely refuse to do after being lodged and fed.

But it was not until the next morning that the minstrels showed themselves again, and then they seemed very shy, Earpwold thought, not at all curious about the place or the people, as strangers usually were.

Osric usually took his meals with the invalid, and so when these had been served, and Earpwold had put his own and the strangers' breakfast on the table, he said, "Before thou dost depart, thou wilt sing to us, Sir Minstrel."

They would have made some excuse if they could, but Earpwold was determined to have something for the trouble they had given him. "Ye are Saxon gleemen, and cannot sing aught fit for the ears of a monk?" he exclaimed.

"Nay, we know but one song fit for these sacred walls, holy father, and that is the song of an Irish, not a Saxon bard."

"Saxon or Irish, it is alike to me, so thou dost sing," said Earpwold.

Finding there was no escape, one of the minstrels began tuning the harp, while Earpwold ran to tell Egbert that the minstrel was about to sing.

"We will open the door, to hear more clearly," said Osric, who knew Egbert's love of music; and as he spoke a faint trembling voice began to sing the hymn of St. Bridget.

Egbert started up in bed at the first sound. "Hush, monk!" he said; and then, as the singing went on, and the minstrel gained confidence, he said, "Osric, Osric, it is my sister—my sister Thyra; she hath followed us, she is determined to leave the world."

"It were better for her to abide at home," said Osric, with some vexation; and he called Earpwold, to question him about the minstrel.

"Didst thou not tell me there were two glee-men?" he said, rather sharply.

"Yes!" answered Earpwold; "thou canst see them for thyself."

"But one of them is a woman," said Osric.

Earpwold could only stare, and wonder whether Osric had learned the Danish magical arts since he had been among them; for it was strange that he should know so much about a person he had not seen. But Egbert's next words explained the mystery.

"Nay, nay, she is my sister, Osric, and would fain become like St. Bridget. She doth desire to know and serve God; and how can she do this in such a home as ours, or with such a man as my father would fain force her to wed?"

"But—but what will she do here?" asked Osric, in perplexity; for he had mentally vowed never to see or speak to a woman again if he could help it, and also that he would protect his brethren from such a temptation as he had fallen into; and this he was determined to do, cost what it would.

When Thyra was brought to her brother's bedside, she burst into tears. "Oh, Egbert, what is it? What hath happened?" she asked.

Egbert explained as well as he could, and then Osric asked, rather sternly, why she had come into East Anglia, and who her companion was.

"She is my cousin—my cousin Ethelfleda," stammered the poor girl.

"Two—two women," uttered Osric; and he looked at Egbert, and then at Thyra, wondering how he was to get out of this dilemma.

"Why didst thou leave my uncle's house, and wherefore did Ethelfleda leave her home?" asked Egbert.

"Because, like me, she doth long to serve God rather than men; but my uncle, who knoweth nought of this, would fain force her to wed a Danish ealdorman."

"And Ethelfleda hath refused!" said Egbert and Osric in a breath.

"How could she wed a pagan?" said Thyra.

Osric looked at Egbert in silence for some minutes, and then he said, "This will not end thus. Mercia hath given offense to East Anglia in this matter, and in searching for cause of quarrel this will be found, and Ethelfleda's scorn will be terribly avenged."

Chapter XIX

Dark Fears

IT was easy to see that Osric looked upon the coming of Thyra and Ethelfleda as a great calamity, and there were several anxious consultations held with Egbert before it could be decided what they should do. At length it was settled that now Egbert was getting better he should teach his sister and cousin to read, while Osric devoted more of his time to teaching and preaching to the people of the town. The songs of Cædmon won him a hearing in Broderickworth, as they had in Ea; and then Osric would go a little further, and tell the story of God's loving-kindness and tender mercy in sending His Son Jesus Christ to die for men.

While Osric was thus teaching and preaching in the town, Egbert was no less busily employed; for neither his sister nor his cousin could read, and he had resolved that they should learn this art, as well as the Lord's Prayer and Apostles' Creed, which was all Osric thought they ought to be taught at present.

Thyra was quite as anxious to learn as her brother was to teach her; for if she was to grow like St. Bridget she must be a useful woman, not a mere hermit. Egbert told her she must learn to read, so that she could teach the little children by and by; and it might be that the homely work of spinning and weaving and sewing, which every Saxon girl learned, would be useful too, he added.

She was in some fear of Osric, for he rarely spoke to her or Ethelfleda, and she feared he did not like their coming to Broderickworth. One day she said something of this to her brother, but Egbert put aside the question by saying, "Nay, but thou knowest all monks care little for women, and therefore when ye come to the hermitage ye must see to it that ye avoid all the brethren."

"We will not come, an thou thinkest it were not well," said Ethelfleda.

"Why! wouldst thou return home again?"

"Nay, nay, we desire above all things to serve God, and how can we serve Him in the world? Let us go to this hermitage, and dwell together, and it may be that by and by others will come to us there, and we may help ye monks a little in teaching these Danes."

Egbert almost wished that the girls had grown tired of their present mode of life, and that the loneliness had already made them wishful to return; but since this was not so, he could not urge it upon them.

The summer had begun to wane before Egbert
was well enough to journey on to Ea, and by this
time the people had grown to like their teachers:
since there seemed to be little hope of their king
leading them out on another campaign, they readily agreed to sow their fields with corn; for if they
could not go out pillaging their neighbours, they
must soon starve, unless they sowed and reaped
for themselves.

It was some comfort to Osric that the summer's
work was not quite in vain, but he felt bitterly disappointed that the church had not been built at
Eglesdune, and he told Egbert of the finding the
grave of the martyr-king Edmund.

"And thou sayest miracles have been wrought
by the body of the saint," said Egbert, when he
had heard the wonderful story; "nay, then his
body should not remain buried in this little village; it were well to remove it from thence to some
place of safety. And since this monastery of Broderickworth is a great and noble building, and hath
been spared by the Danes, would it not be well to
remove it hither? and all the brethren might come
and dwell in this place and guard the precious
relic."

But Osric shook his head. "Nay, my brother, such
a relic as the body of St. Edmund is too precious
to be entrusted to any building yet. In the ground
it is safe from fire and destruction; but by and
by, perhaps, when the Dane-folk are more settled,

and are Christians by choice as well as by charter, it were well perhaps to carry it to Thetford or Broderickworth, but we must not be in haste to do this."

As they drew near Ea, Osric said, "I would that I could have been at the chrism-loosing of Thorgiva and her brother."

"Well, since thou wert not here, wilt thou not take some of the things I have brought, that thou mayest give them the usual gifts?" said Egbert.

Osric hesitated for a moment, but at length he said, "I will take the silver cup thou didst offer me, and this shall be for the baptismal and wedding gift for Lodbrog and Elswitha. For Thorgiva thou shalt give me a piece of the linen thou hast, an thou wilt."

Egbert and Osric were most joyfully received by Redwald and the other brethren, who had spent their hours of recreation for some weeks in finishing and furnishing one room in the little abbey as a scriptorium or library. A cell had also been prepared for Egbert, and furnished with a few more comforts than fell to the lot of the other brethren; all the crevices in the walls having been carefully filled with clay and moss, and a bedstead raised a little way above the ground, and some skins placed upon it, to serve for bed and covering.

When Osric had asked how all things prospered, and the brethren had knelt together in the little church to join in the worship of God once more, he took the presents Egbert had given him, and hastened to the village; for he would fain see for himself whether all things were going smoothly.

To Thorgiva he would go first, and hear from her as much as he could. But he hardly needed to be told that a gradual change was coming over the Dane-folk, for he could see it in the fenced and cultivated fields, and the little patches of garden that a few of the more ambitious had begun to plant.

It was with joyful surprise that Thorgiva met the monk, for she had penetrated his secret before he knew it himself, and she feared that by removing Elswitha to the village again she had given mortal offense to all the brethren.

But Osric met her now with his usual kindness, and asked after her baby and Elswitha, and presented her with the piece of linen, as though nothing had happened.

While Thorgiva was telling him about her baby, and how he grew, and that he could almost walk alone, Elswitha came in, and soon afterwards Lodbrog followed.

Osric started to see Elswitha, but to his surprise he found she was much the same as when she lived in the forest. She went directly to Thorgiva's baby, and took him in her arms, saying, "We have missed thee sorely, holy father; but we should have missed thee more if God had not sent us so many messages of love through this our baby teacher."

"And Elswitha to translate them," said her husband, who had entered while she was speaking.

He looked keenly at Osric; for he had guessed the motive that had somewhat prompted his opposition to their marriage. But he could make more allowance for him than his sister could. The more he knew of Elswitha, the less he wondered that the monk should not think him good enough for her; and he could measure something of his disappointment, by his wife's sweet, gentle, womanly ways, and the simple childlike faith and trust with which she looked up to God. Truly this Christianity was fit for women, since it had made his Elswitha the sweetest and best woman in the Danelagh. But while he thought that all women should learn the secret of this Christianity, and become Christians, he had grave doubts as to its fitness for men. They must be brave, and able to endure anything and everything: and so it was with a keen searching gaze that he looked at the monk now, as though he would read his thoughts and all that was passing in his mind.

Osric was a man, tall and stalwart as himself, and Lodbrog read in his face that there had been a struggle, a long and bitter struggle, before he could bring himself to consent to their marriage. Trying to think what he would have done in the monk's place, had he been put to such a test, he could not but own that his conduct would have been very different. He would have carried off

Elswitha at all costs; would have used all the power
he possessed, spiritual and temporal, to have prevented her marriage. But beyond that first brief
opposition, Osric had not even sought to hinder
it, and Lodbrog felt that it was because he was a
Christian that he had thus gained the victory over
himself, and so Christianity must be as good and
helpful to men as to women. His question was answered, and he resolved to give more earnest attention to the teaching of his wife than he had yet
done. He was amazed that Osric could not only
forgive him the disappointment he had caused,
but could present him with a costly gift; and the
silver cup was enhanced in value tenfold. He was
convinced that if Elswitha was a woman of a thou-
sand, no man who was not a Christian could have
acted as nobly as Osric had in this matter.

This undercurrent of thought went on in Lodbrog's mind while he was talking to Osric, telling
him the news of the village, and all that had happened during his absence.

"Haco, our earl, hath gone to take a Saxon wife
out of thine own kingdom of Mercia, so we have
not gathered in the mead-hall of late," said Lodbrog.

"A Saxon wife!" repeated Osric with a start,
as he thought of Thyra and her cousin. Could it
be from Haco the earl of Ea that either of these
had fled? If it were, and he came back without his
promised bride, it would not be safe for the girls

to abide at the hermitage, or for them to remain in the neighbourhood much longer. Their mission to East Anglia too would be at an end, even if they escaped with their lives, and a campaign against Mercia would be sure to follow such an insult as this.

Osric paid little heed to what he heard afterwards, and he hastened home with all speed to tell Egbert and the brethren the news he had heard, and consult with them as to what had better be done in this fresh dilemma.

"I counsel that we wait until the thane shall return," said Redwald; "it may be that God hath touched his heart, since he doth desire a Christian wife; and if it be so, he will not visit upon us the willful perversity of a foolish maiden."

"Nay, nay; say not that my sister's desire to devote her life to God is willful perversity," put in Egbert, quickly.

"It would be wisest, I think, for thee to see thy sister about the matter. She can doubtless tell us whether the Danish ealdorman of whom she spake was Earl Haco," said Osric.

Egbert bowed his head. "I will see her; but it was Ethelfleda, my cousin, who was to wed a Dane. It may be we are troubling ourselves without cause," he added.

He devoutly hoped it might be so; and, to relieve the brethren's anxiety, he went at once to the hermitage to ask Thyra about this, for at Osric's express desire he rarely saw his cousin now. These two Saxon ladies were as busy in their way as the brethren at the abbey. Whatever time they might have to spare for idle contemplation by and by, the present was fully occupied; for they did not mean to be a useless burden upon the hands of the monks, but rather a help to them: and so the knowledge they possessed of the useful qualities of herbs and roots was being turned to account, and they were gathering and drying these, to be made into medicines or stored for a winter supply to make savoury soups.

Ethelfleda had gone to some distance in search of a rare herb they felt sure would be found in the wood, and which they needed for the proper compounding of a certain popular medicine, but Thyra was sitting sewing at the door of the hermitage when Egbert got there.

She ran to meet her brother the moment she saw him, and displayed with some pride their collection of roots and herbs that were spread to dry in the sun.

"If there should be sickness in the village, thou mayest send the poor women to us," said she. Then suddenly noticing her brother's silence, she whispered, "What is it, Egbert? art thou not pleased that we want to follow the example of St. Bridget?"

"Is St. Bridget the only Christian woman in the world, think you?" asked her brother.

Thyra looked at him in astonishment. "She is the only woman I have heard of, and the gleeman told me he knew of no other," answered Thyra. "Oh, Egbert! thou art not going to turn against us, and bid us give up this life, as brother Osric would do?" she said, clasping her hands.

"Nay, nay, do not cry, Thyra; I have always defended thee; but it may be that we shall all have to fly from Ea, an it be as brother Osric fears. Dost thou know who it was Ethelfleda was to marry, my sister?" he asked, anxiously.

"Earl Haco the Dane," replied Thyra.

"Earl Haco the Dane!" repeated Egbert, almost staggering, as he leaned against a tree for support.

"What is it? what is the matter, Egbert?" asked Thyra, alarmed in her turn; "art thou ill?"

"Nay, nay," gasped the young monk; "but our mission is ruined, and there is nought for us now but to fly to King Alfred for protection, for Mercia will be ravaged again, and every monastery burned."

"But why? why dost thou fear this, my brother?" asked Thyra, with whitening lips.

"Because Earl Haco is ealdorman of Ea, and will surely revenge this insult offered to him."

"And thou dost think he will come and carry off Ethelfleda by force to his mead-hall?" asked Thyra, thinking she might share a similar fate, if her disappointed Saxon bridegroom could only find out where she was hiding.

"Nay, nay; we will not suffer that, while a man of us lives: but we must fly from this place ere the earl returns, or vengeance will surely fall upon us."

"What shall we do? shall I go in search of Ethelfleda now, and—"

"Nay, stay here until Ethelfleda doth return, and then tell her all; but wait until I come to thee again, before ye leave this place. I must go now, and consult with the brethren, and we will bring the matter before God in prayer, that He may give us wisdom how to act; and do ye the same. Spend the night in fasting and prayer, and it may be that He will find a way of escape, that our labour here may not be all in vain."

But although Egbert spoke hopefully to his sister he was far from feeling hopeful himself. It was a sore trial of faith to him, and he knew not how he should tell the brethren that their worst fears were confirmed. But it had to be done, for a chapter must be called at once, that they might consult with each other as to the best means to be adopted in this fresh difficulty.

All night did the monks sit up, praying and consulting. At length they decided that Redwald and one of the other brethren should journey to Broderickworth, and meet Haco on his way home. They would be sure to find out from those who were with him what the future intentions of the earl might be. If he intended to avenge the insult, he would not fail to invite the men of Ea to follow his standard; and they would be only too ready to do so, and flight would be the monks' only safety.

Having dispatched Redwald on this business, Osric's next care was for the church at Eglesdune. Egbert was surprised that he should think so much about this just now, and reminded him that if things should be as he feared, he would be obliged to fly from East Anglia before the church could be completed; but Osric shook his head gravely.

"Nay, nay; God will suffer me to do this work, I trow; and then, if need be—nay, why should I say if need be? should I not rather glory to die upon the martyr's grave?"

"But, Osric, it were better that this church were delayed in the building than that thy life should fall a sacrifice to it," said Egbert, who thought they ought to make some provision for the safety of his sister and cousin, and he said as much to Osric.

"Yes, they must be sheltered," said the elder monk; "and I think thou mayest find a shelter for them, Egbert. But I—I must build this church at Eglesdune before I die. Nay, I will beg this of Haco himself, and then, when the last timber is fastened, will deliver myself to be slaughtered on the altar of Odin, if needs be."

Egbert looked puzzled. "Will it not be throwing thy life away?" he said.

For a minute or two Osric looked painfully perplexed, but at last he said, "Thou art very dear to me, Egbert—dearer almost than life itself; and I will tell thee now a secret—a secret thou mayest divulge after my death, but not before. Didst thou never hear the brethren talking among themselves, that they knew not of my home, or country, or kindred—that there was ever a mystery about me that none could solve?"

Egbert scarcely knew what to say, for he had often overheard whispers concerning the mystery that enshrouded Osric's antecedents; but he only said, "It hath troubled me very little to know what thou wert in the past, for thou wast ever kind to me since the day I first saw thee."

"Ah! when I saw thee first, Egbert, I thought that God had wrought a miracle indeed, and that King Edmund himself had been restored to life again."

"Didst thou ever see the saint-king, then?" said Egbert, in astonishment.

"See him! will there ever be a day, an hour in my life, that I shall not see him?" exclaimed Osric, passionately. "Egbert, thou wilt keep my secret, for I must tell thee now. I am a Dane. I was a follower of Ubba, when he came hither to revenge the death of his father Lodbrog, and it was by my hand that King Edmund was slaughtered. Many had fallen beneath my battle-axe, and I had gloried in the number I had slain; but as the saint-king turned his eyes upon me, I felt that I had been pierced with an arrow more sharp than any that had been shot at King Edmund, and turning away I dropped my battle-axe and fled—fled I knew not whither,

ANTECEDENTS: *events of a person's past*

but ever pursued by the king's eyes, until I wished that someone would slay me as I had slain him. At last I met a Christian monk of Mercia, who knew something of our Danish tongue. I was ill then —ill and almost famished, and he took me to the monastery, and taught me to know and love the God of King Edmund. But although I became a monk, and vowed I would go to East Anglia and teach my people to become Christians, I ever kept this secret locked in my own breast, lest the brethren should grow afraid, and turn me out of the monastery. But now, Egbert, now that we are in such fear of Earl Haco, I thought I would tell thee, that thou mayest know God hath power to turn even the hearts of fierce murderous Danes to himself. And if I, who murdered King Edmund, have found mercy, how much more hope is there for Earl Haco?"

Chapter XX

A New Law for the Danes

EGBERT knew not what to say to the strange story of Osric. It seemed incredible that he could have been one of these ruthless Danish soldiers, and yet it explained much that was otherwise inexplicable. Certainly he could not say another word against his desire to raise a church over the remains of the martyr-king, and he was more willing to undertake the journey to Thetford with Thyra and Ethelfleda, where it was thought they could remain in safety, at least for the present, as the king would be bound to protect them.

But it was resolved that they should wait for the return of Redwald before any of these precautionary measures were undertaken; and, as if the monk's suspense should be stretched to the utmost limits, the summer seemed suddenly to leave them, and a fierce storm of wind and rain arose which lasted several days, and prevented all traveling as well as putting an end to Osric's building operations at Eglesdune.

Finding that he could make no further progress with building the church just now, Osric braved the storm and returned to Ea, and as he drew near the abbey he saw a boat some distance up the river, whose crew seemed scarcely able to manage the oars.

He gave the alarm as soon as he got home, and some of the brethren ran down to the shore, to ascertain whether it was any of their own people or strangers; for the little river ran into the sea, and so it might be that these were coming to Ea for the first time. God help them if they were! for the boat was quite unmanageable now, and so it must be as flotsam and jetsam that they would be cast on the shore of the town.

As the monks drew near they saw that the boat was full of people, many of them being women and little children; and those standing near him saw it too, and were calculating how much these might be sold for in the marketplace. It was months since the sea had brought such a prize as this to their shores: never since the monks had been among them had a boat like this been cast at their feet, and they danced and shouted with joy, regardless of the bitter cries of distress not far off, which the wind in fitful gusts brought to their ears. Earpwold turned away at last, for he could not bear the sight any longer. But no sooner did he reach the abbey than Osric sallied forth, after setting the church door wide open, as well as the gates leading to it.

FLOTSAM: *the floating wreckage of a ship*
JETSAM: *the cargo "jettisoned" or thrown off a sinking vessel to lighten the load*

"Some must be rescued," he said, folding his gown closely about him, and drawing the cowl over his head, while he bade Earpwold keep up the fire he had lighted on the hearth in the middle of the refectory.

Halfway down the path he turned back again, to say another word to his companion. "If any come in here, take them to the church, and bid them hold close by the altar until I return."

Then he hurried down to the bank of the river, not merely to note how near the boat was to the shore, but also to look among the crowd to see if Elswitha was there. Yes, there she stood, with a look of agony in her face, her hands clasped, and her eyes strained, in the hope of seeing that the boat would yet right itself, and save its living freight from death or slavery. But the wind roared as loudly as ever, and the blinding rain came down in torrents; so that it was not until Osric touched her on the shoulder that she knew he was near.

In a moment her face changed, and pointing to the boat she said, "Thou wilt save them, holy father?"

But the monk could only shake his head sadly. "Not all, I fear; a few may reach the sanctuary of the church, but thou and thy husband can save some, an thou wilt."

"Lodbrog will do aught thou dost desire," she said, quickly.

"Bid him claim a share for Earl Haco, as well as himself, and give thee the choice."

"And—and whom shall I choose?" whispered Elswitha.

"The women and children," whispered Osric; and the next minute he had thrown aside his cumbersome frock, and was battling with the stream, struggling to reach the labouring boat.

That the monk was about to help the exhausted boatmen to right her, the crowd felt sure, and there were groans and grumblings on all sides; for what right had he to come between them and snatch away their lawful prize when it was almost within their grasp?

Whatever the monk's intentions might have been, they were frustrated; for just before he could reach the boat she gave a sudden lurch, and the next minute all her living freight were struggling in the water.

Of course no one thought of rendering any assistance, except Lodbrog. The onlookers were quietly waiting to seize everything and everybody that the waves brought to them, and there was already some calculation as to the probable number who would be washed ashore, and what quantity of wadmal, grain, and other merchandise, these would be likely to fetch in the market.

Meanwhile Osric had helped two or three to reach the shore: some others who could swim, and in whom the love of life was stronger than the fear of slavery, had also got there, while others, clinging to spars and oars, were drifting in with the tide. Many, who knew all too well what awaited them, quietly sank down beneath the waves, preferring a speedy death to a life of servitude.

Osric himself had a narrow escape from drowning, for in his almost superhuman efforts to rescue the perishing women and children, his own strength became so exhausted that at last he feared he should never reach the shore, when, to complete the disaster, he was suddenly struck by a piece of floating timber, which the angry waves dashed against his head, rendering him quite insensible.

But Lodbrog, who had been anxiously watching the monk for some time, saw the accident, and instantly plunged in to save him from drowning; and when the crowd along the banks saw who it was he was dragging in to the shore, they were ready enough to help, although they had called him thief and meddler only a short time before.

While he was being carried to the abbey, he revived sufficiently to ask, "How many have been saved? Have any gained sanctuary in the church?" and while he spoke two or three half-drowned men rushed past. The sight seemed to renew Osric's strength, and he bade them hasten on with him, as he was anxious to reach the abbey; and when its shelter was gained, he would hardly give himself time to change his clothes and take the necessary refreshments, so anxious was he to go to the church and guard the fugitives from being dragged away by their foes.

He had contrived to make his voice heard while they were in the water, telling them how they might be saved from the awful doom of slavery; and those who had heard the glad news had managed to escape in the confusion that prevailed on the shore.

As Osric had feared, it was not long before a party of Danes made their appearance at the church to claim the fugitives; but he was there to meet them, with the news that they could not, dare not, snatch away those who had sought a refuge at God's altar. They were inclined to laugh at this law of sanctuary at first. Those who were willing even to receive the mercy of God for themselves were by no means disposed to grant it to others, until Osric reminded them of the mighty power that had overwhelmed Pharaoh and his hosts of proud soldiers in the Red Sea, because they would not release their Hebrew slaves from bondage.

He reminded them also of their murder of His chosen servant King Edmund, and how He might bring against them a host far more terrible than Alfred and his men of Wessex, if His law was openly defied, now that His messengers were sent to declare it; until the bold faces almost blanched with terror, and they went off, grumbling still, but quite convinced that it would be madness to provoke such a mighty adversary as this God of love and mercy.

Having secured the safety of those who had fled to the church for refuge, his next care was to collect all the valuables belonging to the abbey—the silver cups, embroidered tapestry, and fine linen brought by Egbert.

True, these had been intended for the decoration of the church, but Osric did not hesitate to take them for a different purpose, believing that he was doing God's service too.

He next went to Lodbrog, who in the absence of Earl Haco was the ealdorman of the town, and soon persuaded him to call a folk-mote the next day, to discuss how these poor creatures who had fallen into their hands should be disposed of.

There had been some grumbling when they were divided, for each man's share would be very small, and comparatively worthless too, for they were mostly women and children, and many of them were sick or had received various injuries in their battle with the waves. There had been no superfluous care taken of any of them, beyond securing them in prison. They had been turned in here, wet, cold, hungry and sick as they were, their captors never thinking it needful to give them so much as a morsel of food.

Elswitha, however, persuaded her husband to let her go with Thorgiva and take some food to the great barn, where they lay huddled together; for the sight of several little children, not much older than her own baby Æthelstan, had touched

FOLK-MOTE: *a general assembly of the people in early England*
SUPERFLUOUS: *unnecessary*

the widow's heart, and she longed to do some-thing for them, and even took some of her own clothes and wraps for the mothers, to make these dry and comfortable, or at least a little less miser-able. Lodbrog would not be seen going himself on such an errand of mercy, but gave Elswitha leave to do as she pleased and take what she liked for their comfort, and then he walked up to the abbey to see Osric, and get out of the way of any remon-strances that his neighbours might be disposed to make at the unusual proceedings of his wife and sister. He really wanted to see Osric too about this folk-mote, and the questions that he had to pro-pose to the assembly.

The monk soon explained his plan, and showed the silver cups and costly embroidery that he proposed to give in exchange; but Lodbrog only shook his head.

"They are ours; our lawful prize, brought to us by the waves; and wherefore wouldst thou take them from us?" he said.

"Lodbrog! thou hast accepted the mercy of God, and called thyself by His name in baptism, and God doth ask thee to show to these, His un-fortunate creatures, the same mercy thou hast thy-self received."

Lodbrog stared. "These be Odin's men; thy God —our God—hath nought to do with these," he said.

"Nay! but our God is king of all the earth, and of all the people who dwell upon it," said Osric,

REMONSTRANCES: *protests*

calmly. And then he explained to his new convert how and why God demanded that mercy should be extended to such unfortunates as these shipwrecked people.

But Lodbrog only seemed half-convinced. He could not give up such a congenial and profitable belief as the sovereign and unalterable rights of flotsam and jetsam, and asked rather discontentedly what Osric proposed to do with the captives, if the people were willing to take the silver cups in exchange.

"Nay! canst thou ask this, Lodbrog? Dost thou need to be told that we will set them at liberty; let them go home; we do not hold slaves."

"But these have no homes; they are part of a fleet of long ships that have come from Daneland with all the people of their town. The soldiers and all the other boats have been driven by the wind they know not whither—flotsam and jetsam like themselves, to be sold in the market; and why should not these?"

"Because God hath commanded us to show mercy to all," reiterated the monk; but at the same time he hardly knew what to do with these men and women, if they were left upon their hands, as they would be should Lodbrog's story prove a true one. It was very likely to be so, he knew, for the Danes frequently left their native land in this way, the whole population of a district, men, women and children, taking to the boats, and steering for some more favoured region than their own cold

North: and wherever they might land the inhabitants must give way, to make room for the invaders. These emigrations had become more frequent since England had been discovered as such a convenient El Dorado; and it mattered little to these roving marauding parties of Danes, whether it was their own countrymen who had got there before them, and held the coveted possession, or people of an alien nation—they were ousted if possible. If they proved the weaker of the two, they neither asked nor expected mercy. They were slaughtered or enslaved without compunction.

This was what would have followed if the whole fleet of boats had sailed up the river to Ea. They would have anchored not far from the shore, and with their wooden shields placed close together, so as to form an almost impenetrable rampart, would have showered a deadly flight of arrows at those who attempted to oppose their landing, and under cover of this attack from their archers the soldiers would land with spear and battle-axe, slaughtering many, before they could recover from the panic caused by the sudden appearance of their foes.

Then there would be a battle, and if the inhabitants were conquered, the abbey and church would most likely be burned down and the monks murdered, unless they could creep away and hide in the wood. After remaining for a little while, perhaps, the newcomers would find the place did not suit them, or they would grow tired of being

El Dorado: *an imaginary city of gold*

on land, and take to their boats once more, carrying away all the valuables they had found, and the best of the captives; while the old and infirm would be left to starve amid the ruins of the homes the invaders had destroyed. Then the fugitives who had escaped would creep back again, and the first among these would be a priest or monk, who would gather the few scattered people he could find, and help them to take heart and lay hold of life once more, by reminding them of the Friend in heaven to Whom their sorrows were not unknown. A few huts would be raised first, and then a temporary church, until times grew better, and their numbers increased.

Osric, knowing the habits of his countrymen, could only feel thankful that Ea had escaped such destruction. But what were they to do with these waifs and strays of the marauding party, who had probably been hopelessly scattered by the storm? Their friends and relatives had most likely been drowned or enslaved, and they had no home to which they could return. They were mostly women and children too; what could they do with them, if they redeemed them from slavery?

It was a perplexing question, so perplexing that Osric was inclined to let matters take their ordinary course, for trading in slaves was such a common thing at that time, only the monk wanted to teach these Danes to show that mercy to others which God required of them.

So he went to the folk-mote on the following day with something less of his usual ardour, although he carried the silver cups and embroidery ready to exchange for the unfortunates; though what he was to do with such a helpless burden upon his hands he did not know.

Lodbrog stated the errand upon which the monk had come, showed his neighbours what the monk proposed to give, told them the probable worth in cattle, grain, or wadmal, their usual articles of barter, and also what the women and children would possibly bring of the same goods. They would be the losers by taking the cups in exchange. And then they asked what Osric wanted these for—the Church had claimed the most valuable portion of the crew in her right of sanctuary.

When Osric explained that he only wanted to set them free—to send them home to their friends, if possible, the people stared at the unheard-of proposal, as though they thought he must be mad; and if it had been anyone but Osric, they would have said he was trying to overreach them, and make a good bargain for himself. But they knew the monk better. Unheard of as it was, they believed in him; and after a little stormy discussion with Lodbrog, they yielded, and Osric went home, with the additional burden of about thirty women and children to provide for, and at present he had not a roof to shelter them.

Chapter XXI

Flotsam and Jetsam

OSRIC soon found, after questioning the men who had taken refuge in the church, that Lodbrog's account was correct, and so for the present the whole party must remain at Ea, and the brethren must support them as best they could.

The first thing to be provided was a house for the women and children, and Egbert at once proposed that this should be built near the hermitage, that his sister and Ethelfleda might do something towards civilizing these half-wild women of the North during their stay, and teach the children if possible.

So the rescued men were set to work to fell and split trees, and build some strong commodious huts round the hermitage, leaving that as the central building for the accommodation of Thyra and Ethelfleda. In the anxiety and confusion consequent upon this shipwreck on their shores, the important errand of Redwald to Broderickworth was almost forgotten, until he suddenly appeared

COMMODIOUS: *spacious*

among them, looking very much surprised at the bustle and active preparation for building instead of flight. The wet weather had detained him, but now that the roads were once more passable, he had pressed on with all speed, to give notice of the approach of Haco.

"What hast thou heard, my brother?" asked Osric, anxiously.

"That he is married, and bringing home his bride," answered Redwald.

Osric breathed a sigh of relief, but he was not quite satisfied yet. "Who is the bride?" he asked, still a little anxious as to what their fate might be.

"Nay, I could not find out more than this—that she is a Saxon lady of Mercia, and a Christian."

"Then she will protect our church and abbey, and, I doubt not, lead Haco fully to embrace our faith," said Osric; and he turned to the work of building with redoubled energy.

The cluster of buildings round the hermitage formed a group almost as large as the abbey itself, and there was little fear now but that the cousins would find ample occupation; for some of the women and children were still suffering from their wounds and exposure, and needed careful nursing. Then everything available had to be made up into garments for them, and Osric, as he occasionally caught a glimpse of one or the other as he was busy in the neighbourhood, wondered what they should do now without these gentle, docile, pious women: they were little more than girls, but so devoted in their earnest endeavour to serve God, and help all who stood in need of help, that they were eager to do anything and everything that was suggested to them; and they were so deft and handy in tending the sick and nursing the children, and preparing herb-tea, and various other decoctions, that the monk quite repented of the hard thoughts he had indulged concerning them. But he wisely kept these thoughts to himself, and still observed most strictly the rule he had laid down for the protection and guidance of himself and the rest of the brethren. No communication was to be held with the women of the community—for that they must form one community was inevitable under the circumstances, at least for the time; and it was no uncommon thing either in those days, indeed it often happened, that a woman was at the head, as in the case of the venerable Abbess Hilda of Whitby. But still the communication between the two was most restricted and stringent, and so Osric made the rule that all business communications should be transacted between Egbert and Thyra, and that the rest of the brethren should not approach that portion of their domain after the new buildings were completed.

They were finished, and the women had just taken possession of their new houses, when news came that Earl Haco had at last arrived, and

DECOCTIONS: *extracts obtained by boiling down*

desired to see Osric at once in the mead-hall, before he called a folk-mote of the people.

Osric was a little alarmed when he received the message. Could it be that he had tracked the fugitives, and knew they were in the neighbourhood?

Lodbrog, who brought the message, either did not or would not know what his chief meant to do at the folk-mote; but his bride had already won for herself a place in the hearts of his house-carles, he said; for, seeing how ragged their clothes were, she and her bower-maidens had already set to work to make them some new ones, so that she was evidently quite willing to take up the onerous duties attaching to the wife of a chieftain.

Osric was glad to hear this; but still he did not quite get rid of his fear, until he reached the mead-hall and Haco fetched his bride from her bower, and presented her to the monk; and then, to Osric's surprise, he saw it was Ethelfleda's sister.

Haco burst into a loud guffaw, and rolled himself back with laughter as he saw the monk's look of astonishment, while the girl-wife, still "in her hair," or, as we should say, "in her teens," blushed and hung her head for a moment, almost hiding her sweet face behind her wealth of golden hair; for, contrary to all custom, Haco had most peremptorily forbidden it to be cut off or hidden away out of sight.

As soon as Osric had sufficiently recovered from his astonishment, he offered the usual

ONEROUS: *difficult, unpleasant*
PEREMPTORILY: *allowing for no contradiction*

congratulations, and then Haco said good-hu-
mouredly, "Ah, monk! but for thee, our Danelagh
would have been ringing with war-shouts, and
there would have been few white shields in East
Anglia at the next Al-thing, for I should have led
all the heroes who would have followed me to Mercia, to avenge the insult this lady's sister hath done
me."

"Nay, nay, Haco," whispered his wife, lifting her
fair face, and looking in his bright blue eyes, that
for a moment gleamed angrily even now.

"There! I'll not grieve thee, little one: I have the
best of the bargain after all, and I would not have
thy sister Ethelfleda an she begged me."

"Poor Ethelfleda!" sighed her sister; "I would
that I knew where she and Thyra had gone."

Osric knew not what to do; but Haco gave him
no time to speak, but said, "Well, monk, if thou
hadst not come here, and taught me and my people thy Christianity, I should not have this fair Saxon wife; for she, like her sister, would have refused
me, had I not told her that I and my people had
given up the worship of Odin, and were learning
to be Christians: and now I have sent for thee, to
ask thee to teach me somewhat more of thy faith,
that I may be baptized, as I have promised the little wife. I may not do this without the consent of
my people, therefore have I called a folk-mote; but
since Lodbrog and Thorgiva his sister have struck
hands with the White Christ, and many come to

the church now, I doubt not they will be willing that I should lay hands in those of this great God of King Alfred, and swear to be His man."

It would be difficult to express the deep, heart-felt joy with which Osric listened to these words: for now, with Earl Haco a baptized Christian man, with a Christian wife at his side to guide and influence him, Ea might, nay would, grow to be a little center from which would radiate gentle, merciful, and Christianizing influences all around; so that ere long East Anglia might become of a truth a Christian kingdom.

In his joyful anticipations of the future, he had almost forgotten the present, until he looked at Haco's girl-wife again, and remembered Ethelfleda; and as the earl had been called aside to speak to one of his lithsmen on some business, he took the opportunity of approaching her.

"I have news of thy sister," he said in a low tone as he drew near.

A little cry of joyful surprise startled the dogs that lay about the floor, as the lady clasped her hands and exclaimed, "Oh, tell me where I can find her!"

"What is it, monk?" asked the earl, striding up to where they stood, as he heard his wife's voice.

But before Osric could answer she said, "Oh, Haco! he hath news of Ethelfleda, she is—" and there the lady stopped.

"She is here in Ea," said Osric, quietly.

"Said I not she had followed the monks, when thou didst tell me of their visit?" thundered Haco; "send her here to us, for—"

"Nay, nay, but she hath vowed to give her life to God and His service, and would fain dwell alone, engaged only in works of mercy and charity," said the monk.

"And Thyra, too? hath she vowed to be a nun?" asked the lady.

"Yes! they both desire to imitate the example of St. Bridget, sung of by the gleeman," said Osric.

"Better follow the example of my little Bertha here, and rule some household well, clothing the naked house-carles, as she doth," growled Haco. "Monk, thy religion will come to nought, an thou persuade foolish girls to try to be saints instead of women."

But Osric shook his head. "Nay, nay, our religion cannot come to nought, for it is Divine, though foolish men and women may do much hurt by their mistakes."

"Ah! and there will be no greater mistake made than this—forgetting they are men and women and trying to be something else. See now, this foolish Ethelfleda would have stirred up strife between two kingdoms, in her hurry to be a saint, if her sister had not been a better one than she."

"Nay, nay, I am not better; I am not good like Ethelfleda," hastily interrupted the lady. "Thou dost know how carefully she treasured every word spoken by some monks who came to breakfast one morning, and said they were going to teach the Danes of East Anglia."

Osric smiled as he said, "I recollect how earnestly thy sister listened to the reading of the Scriptures."

"And thou wast one of those monks?" said Bertha, who had not recognized him before. "My sister never forgot that visit," she went on, "but whenever we were alone she would talk of the monks and their errand, and wish that she too could go to East Anglia and teach the pagan Dane-folk."

"But she would not come to teach me," laughed Haco.

"Nay; but she knew not that thou wouldst prove so gentle a pupil," said the lady, looking up timidly at her lord. "She wanted to be a nun too, and was determined upon this after the minstrel came who sang about St. Bridget."

"Well, now she can have her wish, to be a nun and teach the Dane-folk, and thou mayest help her an thou wilt; but mind, thou art not to be a nun," he added.

Bertha laughed at the threatening little finger held up to warn her; but she was very glad of the permission to help her sister, for doubtless she would be able to do this in many ways, and she too might help in some humble fashion to do the work Osric and her sister had devoted their lives to accomplish.

As the monk returned homewards there was but one thought that lessened the joy with which his heart was overflowing, and that was the recollection that Ea was not Eglesdune. The church there still remained unfinished, and the martyr-king's grave almost unknown; and as he thought of this, and all he had heard at the mead-hall, and looked round now on their well-drained abbey lands, and the substantial timber church and adjacent buildings, he felt that his work in Ea was done. The brethren could spare him now, and Eglesdune lay nearer his heart than any other spot in the wide world. He would go there and finish building the church, and then raise for himself a little cell, where he might spend the rest of his days in penitence and prayer for the sins of his life.

When the brethren heard this they were deeply grieved, and implored him to give up his purpose; but Egbert, who knew the secret of his life, said not a word. He would miss his wise counsels and fatherly advice more perhaps than any of the brethren, but all he said was, "Thy work is not done, brother Osric. Thou wilt not forsake us, because thou art to be a hermit. Thou wilt pray for us still, for the work here hath but just been begun, and we shall sorely need thy prayers, and thy counsel too, in times of difficulty and danger." For Egbert had shown himself wise and skillful, and had been chosen to succeed Osric as the leader of the mission at Ea.

"My poor prayers, thou knowest, will be ever that the work of God here may prosper, and my counsel thou shalt have, if it be needful; but danger cannot—"

"Nay, nay," interrupted Egbert; "dream not that the Dane-folk will give up their old lawless ways all at once. Our work here will doubtless have many interruptions, if it be not wholly ended."

Osric started. "Interrupted it may be, but not stopped—never stopped; the fire on Odin's altar will never be lighted again."

In this the monk was right; the sacred fire was never lighted to any false god in Ea again. The priest of Thor never came back to retard the dawning civilization; and Osric's resolve to spend his life by the grave of the royal martyr, though false in sentiment, was useful in fact; for little Eglesdune became another center from which radiated the light of the Sun of Righteousness.

The monk's active, energetic temperament would never allow him to become a hermit only. Pray he did, and his whole life, since his heart was pierced with that look of the royal martyr, had been one long repentance; but it was not in the man to sit down and indulge it as a mere sentiment. He had drunk too deeply of the spirit of that Master Who spent His whole life in doing good, to sit down a mere idler, and indulge in vague penitence. The needs of the world were too great, too pressing: and so, before his own cell was built, or

RETARD: *hinder*

the tiny timber church finished, a mission was begun there, as it had been at Ea, and men and women were taught to pray at Saint Edmund's shrine, and to serve Saint Edmund's God.

Egbert was nominally the head of the mission at Ea, and at the earnest request of Osric had been named its first prior; but scarcely a week passed without some communication between Ea and Eglesdune, and in every difficulty or perplexity that arose Osric was sent for to counsel and advise, not only by the little communities of monks and nuns, but also by Earl Haco and his freemen.

He would also leave the retirement of Eglesdune, and journey to Thetford, seeking out every little village on his way where he could gather a handful of people to listen to his songs of Cædmon, and so, in addition to the beacon fires kindled at Thetford and Ea, there were little glimmering flames of Gospel light set here and there throughout the length and breadth of the royal martyr's kingdom.

NOMINALLY: *in name*

Chapter XXII

War and Peace

FOR the next year or two all things seemed to prosper in Ea. The more restless spirits took their white shields to France, to win honour and glory at the expense of the Franks instead of the Saxons of Mercia. No one seemed to recognize the danger of thus leaving the little community with few fighting men to protect it against the inroad of an enemy. Osric did counsel that earthworks should be thrown up to guard the town, but Earl Haco had grown somewhat indolent since his marriage, and the Danes soon forgot the shipwrecked boat, that might have brought with it a flotilla of other long ships, filled with fighting men instead of half-drowned women and children. They had done with fighting for the present, and in the new interest of draining, tilling, and fencing their fields, forgot that all their countrymen might not be of the same mind.

A few of the more steady and reliable among them, like Lodbrog, tried to persuade their

INDOLENT: *lazy*

younger neighbours not to go on these marauding expeditions; but their words were unheeded.
Young blood is hot, and the thirst for fighting for
its own sake was unslaked; and although the king,
seeing the prosperity of his town of Thetford since
his people had embraced Christianity, and with it
more settled habits, tried all he could to control
this restless element in the national council, it
proved too strong for him. Although a king, he
was no dictator: the Danes gloried in freedom too
much ever to submit to such a rule, and so after
each Al-thing another army of white shields, attended by a few veterans, for whom civilization
had no charms, set out for some campaign, leaving the more peaceable to return to their homes
and cultivate their fields and gardens.

They were beginning to reap the fruit of their
toil now, in improved dwellings and various comforts and conveniences of life, to say nothing of
the pleasure they found in exercising their su-
perabundant energy in the struggle with nature.
The little town of Ea bore witness to this, in the
timbered dwellings and tidy gardens and well-
drained fields, that stretched to the very edge of
the forest. Here each evening might be heard the
tinkle of the vesper bell, calling the men from
the fields and the monks to prayers, and Sunday
was observed as a day of rest from earthly toil,
even if all did not go to the little church on the
hill.

UNSLAKED: *unsatisfied*

There was still plenty for the monks to do; for men are slow in learning spiritual truth; and it was hard, very hard, for these Danes to practice that "peace on earth and goodwill towards men"[1] which the Gospel commands, even towards their neighbours, and which no outward profession of Christianity could bestow.

Little disputes and jealousies were constantly arising, and in nothing were these more apparent than in the building of the earthworks for the protection of the town. They were finished at last; but the work, grudgingly done, was ill-done; and Osric, as he examined them one day, hoped that there would be no need to test their strength.

But alas for his hope! When Egbert got up one morning, a few weeks after the return from the Al-thing, he saw to his dismay that the little river was full of Danish long ships as far as the eye could reach.

They must have crept up silently by the light of the moon, for the sun had scarcely risen yet, and here they were, putting themselves in battle array, and preparing to land, while the little town was still fast asleep! This sight almost froze his blood with horror, as he looked from the eye-hole of his cell. Scarcely waiting to put on his frock, he called Redwald and dispatched him and the other monks to arouse the town and summon Earl Haco, while he ran to warn his sister and cousin, that they might fly with the women who were with them to

[1] LUKE 2:14

Eglesdune, where Osric might be able to find them a refuge or help them forward to Thetford, if that should prove necessary. This would leave the hermitage, as it was still called, vacant for the women and children of the town; and Egbert hastened there with all speed to bid them get away to this place of safety; for a fight was inevitable, and if the Danes effected a landing they would set fire to the houses the first thing.

The long ships, with their gay-coloured sails and beak-like prows, were in full sight: but the town was aroused, and every man had seized shield and battle-axe, and hastened out for its defense.

The common danger had caused the little quarrels and jealousies to be forgotten, but there was the terrible evidence of them still, in the poor weak earthworks that would certainly yield at the first onslaught of the enemy. Friends looked at each other, and then at the crumbling defenses, but it was no time for recrimination; the long ships with the carved "magic runes" along their sides were close to the shore, and the fair-haired giants, sheltered behind their rampart of overlapping shields, poured a deadly flight of arrows among the little company of defenders. They too were veterans used to warfare, and used the longbow with good effect; but alas! they were far outnumbered by the enemy, and it was all too evident that, fight as they might, the landing could only be postponed, not prevented.

Earl Haco was at their head, and fought with fury, remembering his gentle young wife and tender babe at home. Indeed, every man among them had a dearer self he was bound to defend.

Meanwhile, the monks were not idle. After directing the women to fly for shelter to the hermitage, they packed up all the food and property they could carry, and took it to them. Thorgiva, however, declined to go with the rest of the women. She gave her boy into the care of Elswitha, and arming herself with shield and battle-axe, she went out to help her countrymen in the defense of their homes.

"Our men are few," she said, "all too few, so women must fight." The old Danish spirit was awake in her once more, and she took her place beside her brother Lodbrog, and defended him again and again.

Their only hope lay in keeping the enemy to the boats until help came from Thetford. Osric would send messengers from Eglesdune, telling of what had happened, and the king would get all the men he could muster, and march to their relief as speedily as he could; but twenty miles, even though it was summertime, and the roads were good, could not be traveled in an hour or two, and help would not reach them until the next morning at the earliest.

Earl Haco had taken in the whole situation at a glance. It nerved his arm with fresh strength when

he heard that his young wife with her bower-maidens had followed her sister to Eglesdune, and not
a woman was left in the town.

"Our prior will send to Thetford," he said, "and
if we can but keep these sea-thieves at bay until night, help may reach us in time to save our
homes."

But even as he said this, and looked round at
the handful of men fighting with him, and saw
how many had already fallen, his heart almost
failed him. These could never keep the foe at bay
until night. Stamping his foot angrily, he said,
"We need our white shields to guard our homes
now!"

They fought on—fought like giants, as they were;
but the foe did the same, and with the advantage
of numbers in their favour. At last the townsmen
were driven back, and with a terrific shout of victory the conquerors stepped ashore, and at the
same moment Earl Haco was mortally wounded.

The rest was little more than a triumphant
march into the town, for those of the brave defenders who were not killed were so sorely wounded
that they could do nothing now but watch for an
opportunity to crawl to the forest, and give warning to the women not to venture back.

Lodbrog and his sister were among those who
had been wounded, but not actually disabled from
walking; and when evening fell, and the invaders
were busy feasting and drinking and rifling the

RIFLING: *plundering*

THEY FOUGHT LIKE GIANTS

houses, they crept away from the heap of slain, where they had lain all day, and while the revelry was at its height each began to move towards the forest, both startled a little to see other dead men moving too. But they had not gone far before weakness overcame them, and they would have fallen into the hands of their enemies after all, had not the friendly monks come in search of those still within reach of their help.

Restoratives were given them, and then a little food, and they were helped onward by the kindly brethren. In this way several were saved, who made good their escape to the forest.

The monks did not venture to go back to the abbey or church, but having helped the fugitives to a place of refuge, they concealed themselves in different places,—Redwald to watch the movements of the invaders, and Egbert the road from Thetford and Eglesdune, from whence help might be expected shortly.

He was altogether stronger and more robust than ever seemed possible at one time. Contentment, and the feeling that he was not useless, had given him a fresh hold on life, and he could endure privation and fatigue as well as the rest of his brethren; so he watched for the coming of help, that he might give information as to the state of affairs in the village.

But in the grey dawn of the summer morning came a single messenger through the trees. He

was weary and footsore, but Egbert recognized
him at once.

"Brother Osric," he called from his hiding-place,
and then stepped into view.

"What news, my brother?" asked Osric, eagerly.

"Alas! our enemies have taken Ea, and killed
Haco and most of his freemen. Will the king lead
his heroes from Thetford?" he asked, anxiously.

But Osric shook his head sadly. "There are no
white shields in Thetford," he said, "and many
others have gone on this campaign."

It was a danger none had foreseen, that while
their young men went marauding in some neighbouring kingdom, fresh hordes might come from
the North, to whom those left at home might fall
an easy prey.

Osric told of the consternation that had fallen
upon the men of Thetford when they heard of
what had happened at Ea. But what were they to
do? While they were helping the South-folk their
own homes might fall a prey to another party of
invaders. They offered to receive and shelter the
women and children; but this was all they could
do for their neighbours, and so Ea must be left to
its fate.

Another day passed, the monks and fugitives
subsisting on what they could find about the forest;
for all the women had gone on to Eglesdune, taking the food that was rescued with them. Sounds
of revelry reached them from time to time, and

parties of men had been seen approaching the
church and abbey; but whether they were to be followed by wives and children, and a permanent set-
tlement made here, they could not tell. It was quite
in the order of things that the inhabitants should
be thus dispossessed in turn by fresh troops of
their own countrymen; or they might ravage and
destroy all they could, and then take to their boats
again and sail away with what spoil they had been
able to collect. It was what was being done by the
younger men of this half-settled community on
another shore; and so the evil worked all round.

Events proved that the newcorners had no intention of staying long. They were mere "land-
ravagers," not colonists in search of a more congenial home; and so, after carrying everything
portable to their ships, they set fire to the little
town and the church, and then sailed away again,
after staying about a week in Ea.

As soon as the last boat had disappeared, the
monks crept down to the village. But alas! it was
only a huge blot on the summer landscape; for the
houses were mere heaps of blackened, smoking
ruins. The abbey had been spared, but the church
had shared the fate of the town. Thorgiva and her
brother had followed closely behind the brethren,
and looked on the scene in silent anguish. It may
have occurred to them that they had once gloried
in such hellish destruction; but now all was so
changed, and they had begun to grow so attached

to a settled life, that it was hard to see their homes and fields and gardens ruthlessly destroyed.

"If our white shields had been here, they could have won glory and saved our village too!" said Lodbrog, bitterly.

"Ah! my brother, our young men must abide at home, if there is ever to be prosperity in Ea," said Osric, musingly.

He was wondering how they had better begin to repair the mischief that had been done. The first thing would be to bury the dead, of course, and then he would ask the men of Eglesdune to come and help them put up a few huts. The abbey must be given up to those who had not yet recovered from their wounds, and to the women and children, when they returned from Eglesdune.

Oh! the bitter heartrending cries that went up to Heaven when the survivors, widows and orphans returned once more and gazed on the ruins of their home. It was difficult at first to persuade them to set about the necessary work of clearing and rebuilding. It was of no use, they said; for another band of invaders would come and destroy their homes. But by degrees they took heart, and for the sake of the children struggled to repair the mischief.

But it was still a sadly desolate little town when the warriors returned in the autumn, many of them to find that fathers and brothers and every male relative had been cut off. They swore that they would be revenged at first; but the difficulty was to find the offenders. At last wiser counsels prevailed, and they resolved to go on no more marauding expeditions, but to stay at home and defend their own, should the need arise. It was bitter to hear that if a few more men had been at hand the strangers could not have effected a landing, and the warriors swore they would never leave Ea again, and they kept their promise.

By degrees the old homes were restored, and other homes sprang up beside them. The church was rebuilt, and the little bell rang out its call to prayers once more. The nuns returned to their house, bringing with them the young widow of Earl Haco: for she had declined to return to her father's house, preferring to share the labours and triumphs of her sister and cousin in their work for God among the women and children of Ea.

* * *

So East Anglia was evangelized, and the martyr-king grew to be a saint among his murderers, and thus gained the sublimest victory the world has ever seen. For thirty years his body was allowed to rest where it had first been buried; but as time went on the usurpers of his kingdom grew to reverence him more and more, until at last it was deemed that such an insignificant place as Eglesdune, with its little timbered church and hermits' cell attached, was no fit place for the royal martyr's sepulcher, and so his bones were taken up and re-

SUBLIMEST: *most exalted*
USURPERS: *those who take something they have no right to*
SEPULCHER: *tomb*

moved, with every mark of reverence and honour, to Broderickworth, henceforth to be known as St. Edmund's Bury.

Thus were the Danes won for God, and the kingdom of Christ extended amid many difficulties, many disappointments, many failures, many ebbings of the onward tide; but that it was a flowing, and not an ebb tide, history has long since proved.

Doubtless many grave mistakes were made, and there was much credulity, ignorance, and superstition, which we, from the vantage-ground of our nineteenth-century knowledge, can afford to smile at; but are there no practical lessons for us to learn from these first pioneers of the Gospel? Increase of knowledge brings increased responsibility, but can we compare favourably with these ignorant monks in our zeal for the extension of Christ's kingdom, our love for souls, and self-denying efforts to do good to all men?

Truly these were a royal priesthood in the days of which we write, helping forward the world's progress as no other men could have done; and looking back, we may say, "Wisdom is justified of her children."

THE END

ABOUT THE AUTHOR

Emma Leslie (1837-1909), whose actual name was Emma Dixon, lived in Lewisham, Kent, in the south of England. She was a prolific Victorian children's author who wrote over 100 books. Emma Leslie's first book, *The Two Orphans*, was published in 1863 and her books remained in print for years after her death. She is buried at the St. Mary's Parish Church, in Pwllcrochan, Pembroke, South Wales.

Emma Leslie brought a strong Christian emphasis into her writing and many of her books were published by the Religious Tract Society. Her extensive historical fiction works covered many important periods in church history. Her writing also included a short booklet on the life of Queen Victoria published in the 50th year of the Queen's reign.

Emma Leslie Church History Series

GLAUCIA THE GREEK SLAVE
A Tale of Athens in the First Century
After the death of her father, Glaucia is sold to a wealthy Roman family to pay his debts. She tries hard to adjust to her new life but longs to find a God who can love even a slave. Meanwhile, her brother, Laon, struggles to find her and to earn enough money to buy her freedom. But what is the mystery that surrounds their mother's disappearance years earlier and will they ever be able to read the message in the parchments she left for them?

THE CAPTIVES
Or, Escape from the Druid Council
The Druid priests are as cold and cruel as the forest spirits they claim to represent, and Guntra, the chief of her tribe of Britons, must make a desperate deal with them to protect those she loves. Unaware of Guntra's struggles, Jugurtha, her son, longs to drive the hated Roman conquerors from the land. When he encounters the Christian Centurion, Marcinius, Jugurtha mocks the idea of a God of love and kindness, but there comes a day when he is in need of love and kindness for himself and his beloved little sister. Will he allow Marcinius to help him? And will the gospel of Jesus Christ ever penetrate the brutal religion of the proud Britons?

OUT OF THE MOUTH OF THE LION
Or, The Church in the Catacombs
When Flaminius, a high Roman official, takes his wife, Flavia, to the Colosseum to see Christians thrown to the lions, he has no idea the effect it will have. Flavia cannot forget the faith of the martyrs, and finally, to protect her from complete disgrace or even danger, Flaminius requests a transfer to a more remote government post. As he and his family travel to the seven cities of Asia Minor mentioned in Revelation, he sees the various responses of the churches to persecution. His attitude toward the despised Christians begins to change, but does he dare forsake the gods of Rome and embrace the Lord Jesus Christ?

www.SalemRidgePress.com

EMMA LESLIE CHURCH HISTORY SERIES

SOWING BESIDE ALL WATERS
A Tale of the World in the Church

There is newfound freedom from persecution for Christians under the emperor, Constantine, but newfound troubles as well. Errors and pagan ways are creeping into the Church, while many of the most devoted Christians are withdrawing from the world into the desert as hermits and nuns. Quadratus, one of the emperor's special guards, is concerned over these developments, even in his own family. Then a riot sweeps through the city and Quadratus' home is ransacked. When he regains consciousness, he finds that his sister, Placidia, is gone. Where is she? And can the Church handle the new freedom, and remain faithful?

FROM BONDAGE TO FREEDOM
A Tale of the Times of Mohammed

At a Syrian market two Christian women are sold as slaves. One of the slaves ends up in Rome where Bishop Gregory is teaching his new doctrine of "purgatory" and the need for Christians to finish paying for their own sins. The other slave travels with her new master, Mohammed, back to Arabia, where Mohammed eventually declares himself to be the prophet of God. In Rome and Arabia, the two women and countless others fall into the bondage of man-made religions—will they learn at last to find true freedom in the Lord Jesus Christ alone?

GYTHA'S MESSAGE
A Tale of Saxon England

Having discovered God's love for her, Gytha, a young slave, longs to escape the violence and cruelty of the world and devote herself to learning more about this God of love. Instead she lives in a Saxon household that despises the name of Christ. Her simple faith and devoted service bring hope and purpose to those around her, especially during the dark days when England is defeated by William the Conqueror. Through all of her trials, can Gytha learn to trust that God often has greater work for us to do *in* the world than *out* of it?

www.SalemRidgePress.com

For Younger Readers

DOWN THE SNOW STAIRS
Or, From Goodnight to Goodmorning
by Alice Corkran
Illustrated by Gordon Browne R. I.
On Christmas Eve, eight-year-old Kitty cannot sleep, knowing that her beloved little brother is critically ill due to her own disobedience. Traveling in a dream to Naughty Children Land, she meets many strange people, including Daddy Coax and Lady Love. Kitty longs to return to the Path of Obedience but can she resist the many temptations she faces? Will she find her way home in time for Christmas? An imaginative and delightful read-aloud for the whole family!

SOLDIER FRITZ
A Story of the Reformation
by Emma Leslie
Illustrated by C. A. Ferrier
Young Fritz wants to follow in the footsteps of Martin Luther and be a soldier for the Lord, so he chooses a Bible from the peddler's pack as his birthday gift. When his father, the Count, goes off to war, however, Fritz and his mother and little sister are forced to flee into the forest to escape being thrown in prison for their new faith. Disguising themselves as commoners, they must trust the Lord as they wait and hope for the Count to rescue them. But how will he ever be able to find them?

AMERICAN TWINS OF THE REVOLUTION
Written and illustrated by Lucy Fitch Perkins
General Washington has no money to pay his discouraged troops and twins Sally and Roger are asked by their father, General Priestly, to help hide a shipment of gold which will be used to pay the American soldiers. Unfortunately, British spies have also learned about the gold and will stop at nothing to prevent it from reaching General Washington. Based on a true story, this is a thrilling episode from our nation's history!

www.SalemRidgePress.com

Historical Fiction by William W. Canfield

THE WHITE SENECA
Illustrated by G. A. Harker
Captured by the Senecas, fifteen-year-old Henry Cochrane grows to love the Indian ways and becomes Dundiswa—the White Seneca. When Henry is captured by an enemy tribe, however, he must make a desperate attempt to escape from them and rescue fellow captive, Constance Leonard. He will need all the skills he has learned from the Indians, as well as great courage and determination, if he is to succeed. But what will happen to the young woman if they do reach safety? And will he ever be able to return to his own people?

AT SENECA CASTLE
Illustrated by G. A. Harker
In this sequel to *The White Seneca*, Henry Cochrane, now eighteen, faces many perils as he serves as a scout for the Continental Army. General Washington is determined to do whatever it takes to stop the constant Indian attacks on the settlers and yet Henry is torn between his love for the Senecas and his loyalty to his own people. As the Army advances across New York State, Henry receives permission to travel ahead and warn his Indian friends of the coming destruction. But will he reach them in time? And what has happened to the beautiful Constance Leonard whom he had been forced to leave in captivity a year earlier?

THE SIGN ABOVE THE DOOR
Young Prince Martiesen is ruler of the land of Goshen in Egypt, where the Hebrews live. Eight plagues have already come upon Egypt and now Martiesen has been forced by Pharaoh to further increase the burden of the Hebrews. Martiesen, however, is in love with the beautiful Hebrew maiden, Elisheba, whom he is forbidden by Egyptian law to marry. As the nation despairs, the other nobles turn to Martiesen for leadership, but before he can decide what to do, Elisheba is kidnapped by the evil Peshala and terrifying darkness falls over the land. An exciting tale woven around the events of the Exodus from the Egyptian perspective!

www.SalemRidgePress.com

CPSIA information can be obtained at www.ICGtesting.com
Printed in the USA
LVOW070737240313

325713LV00001B/9/A